SCREAMING DEATH

Frank opened his hand, studying the detonator for a long moment.

"Drop it, I say!" The ragged edge to Habib's voice was far more convincing than the volume he used.

Shrugging, Frank turned his hand, letting the detonator fall.

Passengers screamed as they saw the instrument of their destruction drop to the floor. Even Habib flinched, drawing back from the expected explosion.

Frank used that second to stomp on the detonator, crushing its radio microcircuits. Then he dove for the floor, praying that Joe would take his lead.

THE HARDY BOYS CASEFILES™ NO. 10

HOSTAGES OF HATE

FRANKLIN W. DIXON

GREY CASTLE PRESS

Library edition:
GARETH STEVENS PUBLISHING

First Grey Castle Edition, Lakeville, Connecticut, September, 1988

Published in Large Print by arrangement with Simon & Schuster, Inc.

Printed in the U.S.A.

Library of Congress Cataloging-in-Publication Data

Dixon, Franklin W.
    Hostages of hate.

    (The Hardy Boys casefiles ; no. 10)
    Summary: The kidnapping of Frank Hardy's girlfriend at an antiterror convention in Washington, D.C., sends the brother sleuths running straight into a terrorist deathtrap.
    1. Large type books. [1. Terrorism—Fiction. 2. Mystery and detective stories. 3. Large type books] I. Title. II. Series: Dixon, Franklin W. Hardy Boys casefiles ; no. 10.
[PZ7.D644Hp 1988]   [Fic]   88-21368
ISBN 0-942545-51-6 (lg. print)
ISBN 0-942545-61-3 (lib. bdg.: lg. print)

HOSTAGES OF HATE

Chapter

1

"LOOK AT THIS place. Is it disorganized!" Joe Hardy scowled as he pushed his way through the huge crowd.

"It's all the media people getting in one another's way," his older brother, Frank, replied. They circled around one camera crew, only to walk into another. "But then, I suppose a national seminar on counterterrorism is big news."

The two brothers had taken Friday off from school and were down in Washington, D.C., because their father was taking part in the seminar. A successful private detective, Fenton Hardy was giving a lecture on the latest in security methods. Frank and Joe had gone along to be his friendly audience—and to pick up some new techniques for their own use. Fenton Hardy didn't always approve of their work as detectives, but he didn't forbid them from doing it, either.

Joe ran a hand through his blond hair, his face the picture of frustration. "So far, it's just been a lot of hot air. All talk."

"What were you expecting?" Frank almost laughed. "A bunch of musclemen with Uzis and bazookas, demonstrating them in this crowded room?"

"We could use a couple of demonstrations," Joe said. "Better than listening to some guy talk about"—he pulled out a program—"International Effects of Jungle-based Radical-Liberational Movements." He stared in scorn. "What does that *mean?* How can that help if some crazy throws a bomb . . ." His voice trailed off, and his face went white.

Frank stood silently, his dark eyes full of sympathy. He knew what was doing through Joe's mind. The same picture was going through his: their car blowing up from a terrorist bomb. And Joe's girlfriend, Iola Morton, disappearing in the ball of flame.

"Come on, let's get out of here," Frank said, breaking the mood. "I've had enough classes lately. This is supposed to be a break from school."

They stepped out of the building. Joe took a deep breath of fresh air. "This was what I needed," he said. "I was getting a little crazy in there."

"You know," Frank said, "we're only about a quarter of a mile from the airport. What do you say we take a walk over there?"

Joe grinned knowingly as he looked at his brother. "And why would you want to go over there?" he asked. "As if I didn't know."

Frank looked at his watch. "Well, they're getting ready for the hostage exercise. I thought you might like to see it."

"Wait, wait," said Joe. "I feel a deduction coming on." He stroked his chin and pretended to be deep in thought. "I suspect you have another motive for going there. Someone you want to see."

"Come on," Frank said, complaining. "If we don't get there soon, Callie will be on the plane."

The most publicized part of the seminar was going to be a fully staged airplane hijacking. The "terrorists" would be fake—counterterrorist experts. But the people at the seminar, including all the government officials, were going to treat the exercise as real. They'd be acting out their parts in front of television cameras.

Policemen, security agents, and hostage negotiators would swing into action as if a hijacking were actually taking place. And the plane, pilots, and passengers would be real—ordinary people picked at random from the people at the conference.

One of the passengers was Frank's girlfriend, Callie Shaw, whom Fenton Hardy had invited to join them. "She was so excited to be chosen," Frank said as he and Joe walked to the airport. "All I kept hearing about was what an adventure it would be—how lucky she was."

"Lucky?" Joe laughed. "I don't know about that. She's going to spend hours cooped up in that DC-9. She'll probably be bored to death—if heatstroke doesn't get her first." He grinned. "They turn the air-conditioning off when a plane is stuck on the ground with its engines off. It'll be like a sauna in there."

Frank glared at his brother. "You might have mentioned all this stuff to her, you know."

"What?" asked Joe, all innocence. "And ruin her fun?"

They headed for the airport, but the walk took longer than they had expected. Apparently, preparation for the exercise had created a monumental traffic jam. Even pedestrians couldn't get through the wall of cars.

Frank and Joe ran through the Departures building to Gate 61, where International Airways' "Flight to East Nowhere" was supposed to be leaving. But when they got there, the passenger lounge was empty.

"I'm sorry, sir," said the agent. "All passengers have boarded the airplane."

"I wanted to say goodbye to someone." Frank was very disappointed.

"That won't be possible," said the attendant.

4

"But you can watch the takeoff from the observation deck."

Joe shrugged. "Doesn't sound too interesting to me. We all know the plane is never going to take off."

But Frank surprised him by saying, "Let's give it a try."

They managed to squeeze through the crowd gathered to watch the exercise. They sidled to the front and stood at the huge plate-glass windows of the observation deck, looking down at the International Airways plane. It wasn't the biggest airliner they had ever seen, but it certainly was beautiful. The whole body of the sleek jet was painted royal blue with gold trim. The two jet engines set in the tail of the plane were gold with blue trim.

"What do you expect to see from this far away?" Joe asked.

"You can see a lot—if you come prepared," Frank answered. He reached into his pocket and pulled out what looked like a squat fountain pen. As he pulled on the ends, it telescoped into a miniature spyglass. "One of the surveillance tools they were selling at the seminar," Frank said. "I couldn't resist it."

He scanned the side of the plane. "If I know Callie, she has a window seat."

"What if she got one on the other side of the plane?"

Frank glanced at Joe. "Spoilsport." He went

5

back to looking through his spyglass. "There she is. Up near the front of the plane—first class." Callie's blond hair was unmistakable. So was the lively look on her face as she gazed out the window. Frank raised a hand to wave, then put it down. "She'd never see me."

"Well, you got your look at her," said Joe. "Happy now?"

Frank smiled. "Happy." He was about to put the spyglass away when a flurry of movement caught his eye. The main door of the airplane suddenly pushed out and swung away. A man stood in the doorway. He wore a conservative gray business suit, a white shirt, and a yellow tie. A large black bag with eyeholes cut in it had been slipped over his head. In his hand gleamed an Uzi submachine gun.

"Uh-oh," said Frank. "Looks like the show's starting." He focused in on the supposed hijacker.

The guy was shouting and pointing wildly with one arm. Frank refocused his spyglass to see airport personnel running around on the tarmac. Then suddenly they were huddling on the ground or diving for cover.

Frank flicked back to the guy in the doorway. Sure enough, his Uzi was spitting flame.

"Outrageous!" said Joe, straining to see what was going on. "They're going to use up a lot of blanks in this exercise."

"Hey, look!" Frank said, still scanning the

scene. "The pilot, copilot, and navigator are escaping!" Both crew members had dropped from the cockpit on a rope ladder, then sprinted across the smooth surface. The hijacker turned toward them. He fired a burst as they dove for cover behind a pile of luggage.

Frank froze as he focused on a row of neat holes appearing in the suitcases.

"Something's wrong," he said hoarsely. "That guy is using real bullets!"

Chapter

2

Now Frank could see other evidence that live ammunition was flying over the tarmac. Ricochetted bullets *spanged* off vehicles. A truck's windshield vanished in a spray of gunfire. The driver bolted from the cab, miraculously unhurt.

The gunner wasn't aiming at anything—or anyone—just swinging his Uzi in a half-circle, with steady pressure on the trigger. Frank had just refocused on him when a stray round shattered the window in front of him. Joe yanked his brother back into the crowd pressed close against them. The safety glass crumbled and fell to the floor where they'd been standing.

With the glass gone, they could hear the wild uproar on the runway below. Terrified yells and screams rose from the trapped airport personnel.

Then they were drowned out by the renewed snarl of rapid fire from the Uzi.

Instinctively, Frank and Joe ducked and hit the floor. "The guy must have slapped in a new magazine," Joe said.

Frank aimed his spyglass at the door again, just in time to see the gunman disappear. The reason was obvious—police and counterterrorist experts were charging onto the scene.

Frank and Joe stared as if they were watching a movie. The law-enforcement officials ran back and forth. Some rushed forward, as if to charge the plane. The Uzi snarled again, stitching a line of broken runway just in front of the police. They stumbled to a stop, falling over themselves to retreat in Keystone Kops style.

A voice boomed from the airplane. "You will not come any closer," it announced in lightly accented English. "If anyone passes that line, passengers on this aircraft will die."

Joe turned to his brother, but Frank had shoved his way through the crowd and was dashing from the observation deck. Down on the lower level of the terminal building, police and security people ran around, seemingly without reason. They had all been prepared for a test—but now the test had been turned into a life-and-death situation.

Frank had no problem getting onto the runway himself. And it was no problem for Joe, either, as he pursued his brother.

When they headed for the airplane, however, a large policeman appeared in front of Frank, but he brushed right past him.

That was the worst thing he could have done. The cop, figuring Frank was joining the terrorists aboard the plane, drew his pistol.

Joe pushed himself to top speed.

The policeman, hearing running footsteps behind him, hesitated for a split second and looked over his shoulder. Joe used that time to pass the cop and hit Frank in a flying tackle.

Joe, holding Frank down, explained about Callie to the cop. Then he asked, "Where can we get the story on what's going on?"

The policeman shrugged his burly shoulders. "I wish I knew," he said.

Beyond them, workmen were bringing out sawhorses and boards. The cop glanced over. "Well, somebody's finally getting things organized. They're setting up a police line."

Frank slowly rose to his feet, staring over the improvised barricade to the plane beyond. A crowd was gathering just behind the sawhorses. Not casual bystanders—the police were keeping them away. No, this crowd bristled with microphones and Minicams—newspeople in search of a story.

"We can't find out anything here," Joe said. "Come on. Let's head back to the conference. With all the experts there, that's where the action will be."

Frank nodded and started off, almost robotlike. Joe trailed behind.

When they got back to the conference hall, it was like walking into a circus. There were even more camera crews than before. And standing in front of them were dozens of experts, all giving opinions on the daring hijack.

Joe stared in dismay. "This is even worse than the airport. Nothing's changed. It's just gotten louder."

Frank pointed around the hall. Television sets now dotted the floor, adding to the noise. "Everyone wants to see what the networks have to say about the hijacking."

Joe turned to the nearest set. Washington correspondent Pauline Fox was talking from the barricade by the plane. She was every inch the skilled news professional—her blond hair was perfectly in place, and her voice had just the right note of concern. Rising behind her was the hijacked International Airways plane.

"To recap the story," she said, "a test went disastrously wrong today at National Airport." She stared into the camera. "This airplane full of passengers was supposed to be hijacked today— by government agents, as an exercise for the National Conference on—"

The picture suddenly went wild, jagged bars of color zigzagging across the screen. The uproar in the center grew—every television in the huge room was acting the same way.

Then they all cleared, and every set showed the same picture.

In a dimly lit room, a man sat in an armchair. The semidarkness made it impossible to see his face.

"Good afternoon, delegates to the seminar on terrorism." His English was very precise, but a trace of harshness lingered on the consonants. "The time has come for me to introduce myself. Not personally, of course. Your many law-enforcement agencies are already trying to identify me. I am the leader of the Army for the New World Order. We have taken control of the airplane that was to be used for your test."

Chuckling dryly, the man went on. "I have commandeered all the televisions at your conference. This is so you will know for certain that it is my group in command of the hostages. We were the only ones ready with this particular prerecorded message. I would not want any group of madmen calling the media and claiming responsibility for an act by ANWO."

"Some group of madmen," Joe muttered. "This guy doesn't sound like he's got all *his* screws bolted down too tight."

But the terrorist leader's quiet, clipped voice went on. "It is most important that you understand with whom you are dealing. We are a serious group, and we expect that all of you will treat us seriously. Soon, a videotape of ANWO's demands will be made available to the media. These

12

are unconditional demands, and we do not intend to negotiate."

A chill crept over Frank Hardy's body as he heard the calm voice speaking reasonably about madness and bloody murder. "I most earnestly hope that I can depend on your cooperation."

The leader hesitated for a moment. "Otherwise," he finally said, "I assure you, all of the people on that aircraft will die."

Interference blurred the screens again, then Pauline Fox reappeared.

"That guy is mocking us—right to our faces!" a man burst out. Joe could read his name tag: "R. O'Neill, National Advisory Committee on Terrorism."

Pauline Fox wasn't standing in front of the hijacked plane anymore. She was walking toward it, and the camera was following her. "I've been invited aboard the airplane to meet a spokesperson . . ." Joe caught the words over the uproar.

Professor T. J. Hayden of Hadley University looked disgusted. "Great. They're arranging media opportunities now."

"We should be blacking out this whole thing!" R. O'Neill said explosively.

"And show the world how afraid we are?" asked Hayden. He shrugged. "And if we tried, what do you think the terrorists' first demand would be? With the hostages' necks on the line."

Pauline Fox was actually aboard the plane now, in the first-class cabin. It was empty, except for the armed, masked terrorist in the suit and three passengers. One was a gray-haired elderly man, the second was a woman with carefully arranged orange hair, and the third was a blond young woman. Frank and Joe both gasped. "Callie!"

The camera focused on the elderly man as the terrorist stood behind him. "Professor Beemis, a noted authority on international affairs," came the terrorist's slightly accented voice. "You will tell them about conditions on this aircraft."

"N-no one was hurt as they took over," the professor said shakily. "I don't know about outside—" His voice was cut off abruptly as the terrorist laid a hand on his shoulder.

"Look at that!" O'Neill said. "They're probably talking from a prepared script—and that guy doesn't want the professor moving away from it."

"Professor Beemis," Pauline Fox's voice called out. "Are you—"

"You will ask no questions," the terrorist's voice said. "Otherwise, you will leave."

He moved behind the orange-haired woman. "Mrs. Margaret Thayer, wife of Senator Thayer."

"They've got guns and lots of ammunition." The woman's voice was shrill. "And they've got a bomb in a briefcase. They say it's enough to blow up the plane and kill everyone on it." Tears began to run down her face, streaking her care-

14

fully applied makeup. "I don't want to die! You've got to listen to these people!"

The camera zoomed in on the weeping woman. Then the terrorist moved on to Callie. "Miss Shaw, a student, and the youngest person on the aircraft."

Callie's voice was low and tight as she began. "We've been treated—"

The terrorist's hand landed on her shoulder. "Louder."

She appeared to be blinking away tears as she started again. "We've been treated very well. No one has been mis-mistreated. Our captors—"

O'Neill stood in front of the set. "I can't stand to listen to any more of this."

But Frank pushed him aside. "Quiet." He was staring fixedly at the screen, his lips moving.

"What's the big idea, kid?" The government expert leaned over Frank, who pushed him aside without turning from the TV.

"Callie and I have a system for sending messages to each other across the classroom in school. We blink our eyelids."

"Blink?" Joe repeated. "What kind of messages?"

Frank's ears turned red, but he didn't look at his brother. "Not as important as this one." He read from the screen: "Frank. Only two on plane." He paused for a second. "Help."

Callie's voice went on, parroting how well the terrorists were treating them.

"Just two guys holding all those people," Joe said.

Callie's eyes blinked again. "Bomb real," Frank read. His hands clenched into fists.

As her speech finished, the camera pulled back from Callie. "I have something to add," the terrorist said, still standing behind her.

The camera switched to the masked face. With the black bag over his head, he looked almost laughable—except for the cold stare coming from behind the eyeholes.

"We have one further message for the government of the United States," he said. "We are fighting a war and are willing to die for our cause. We will also execute all enemies—man, woman, or child."

The camera pulled back to show that the terrorist had pointed the barrel of his Uzi at Callie's head.

"We regret this demonstration, but your government must be made aware of our seriousness . . ." The man's hand tightened on Callie's shoulder as he aimed the gun.

"Oh no," Joe breathed.

"*NO!*" The cry was torn from Frank as he leaped at the set.

But even as he moved, the picture disappeared. The screen went blank.

Chapter

3

ABOARD THE PLANE, Callie Shaw shut her eyes and struggled not to let her fear show on her face. These guys will never see me cry, she promised herself. And they won't see me beg.

Behind her, she heard the terrorist's voice. For once, it wasn't full of icy confidence. "What? What are you doing?" he cried, surprised.

Callie opened her eyes to see Pauline Fox standing beside her cameraman. "I turned off the camera," the newswoman said. "Our live feed is off—there are just blank screens out there now." Her voice shook as she glared at the terrorist. "I will *not* stand here and film a murder for you."

The gun muzzle at Callie's head quivered with the terrorist's annoyance. "You will show what we tell you to show."

"No," said Pauline Fox.

"You are a news broadcaster," said the gunman. "You are supposed to report the news." He gestured at Callie. "This is news."

"It's cold-blooded killing. And I won't play a part in it."

"We could get other newspeople in here—" The terrorist's voice was cold and confident again.

"Not after what just went out," Pauline Fox retorted. "They know what you're up to. Nobody will give you live airtime."

The terrorist stood for a long moment, his gun still resting against Callie's temple. Then the cold metal left her head. "Into the other cabin," he ordered abruptly.

Professor Beemis and Mrs. Thayer hurriedly got to their feet, scuttling for the cabin door.

Callie turned back at the door to see that the gun was now aimed at Pauline Fox and her cameraman. "You too, Miss Fox."

A hand grabbed Callie by the hair, hauling her into the economy cabin of the plane. "Inside, you," a voice screamed in her ear.

She turned to look into the second hijacker's face, which was not protected by a mask. His dark eyes were level with hers as he dragged her along—he was only as tall as she was. But he had a wiry strength and a machine gun in his hand—she wouldn't argue with him.

The man's eyes burned like coals against the dark tan of his face, his coarse black hair dancing wildly as he pushed her down the aisle. The tan business suit he wore was now blotched with sweat stains at the back and under the arms. "Sit here," he shouted, thrusting her into an aisle seat.

Callie glanced around the semidarkened cabin. All the window shades were down, to keep the police from seeing what went on inside. The men on the plane had been put in the window seats. Some of them nursed bruises where the terrorists had hit them. "Neutralizing them," the gray-suited terrorist had called it. Breaking their spirit is more like it, Callie told herself. Showing them that two guys with guns can beat up a planeful of unarmed men.

Only women were now sitting in aisle seats. They figure women are too weak to attack them as they pass in the aisles, Callie realized. She watched the man's back. Maybe I'll have a chance to give them a nasty surprise.

The tan-suited terrorist walked up and down the aisle, his Uzi at the ready. He whirled around when the other terrorist entered the cabin—with Pauline Fox ahead of him. The cameraman had been locked in the cockpit.

"Calmly, Habib," said the gray-suited gunman as his comrade's gun snapped into firing position.

"Do not think this is his real name. We use false names."

"What is she doing here?" Habib yelled, anger thickening his accent. "Lars, I do not have my mask."

"It is necessary." Lars pulled his mask off too, revealing a pale face that looked as if it had been chiseled from ice. Handsome as that of a statue, and with about as much feeling. His eyes were like twin blue pebbles as he looked at his partner.

"Miss Fox will not cooperate in transmitting all of our message."

"That's *Ms*. Fox, and I won't—" The rest of Pauline Fox's words were cut off as Habib charged down the aisle and pointed his gun at her. The muzzle was only inches from her face.

"You will do this thing!" His voice was almost a scream.

Pauline Fox stood very still as she stared at the gun. Even though her face was pale, she shook her head. "No."

"I will kill you then!"

Then Callie called out, "You do that. And you can kiss goodbye any hopes of getting your precious message out."

Habib whirled around, ready to smash his gun into Callie's face. But the blue-eyed man reached over to grab the other's arm. "Why do you say that?" he asked Callie.

"The newspeople won't give you a second on television if you kill a reporter."

The cold blue eyes narrowed, considering that fact. Then they turned and gave Pauline Fox an appraising look. "You are a brave woman to refuse us even after we have threatened you. So I will no longer threaten *you*. But what happens if I threaten someone else?"

Pauline glanced at Callie, but the gray-suited man shook his head. "I was thinking about your cameraman. We could execute him instead of Miss Shaw. It would not be a problem."

"But how can you shoot the cameraman?" Callie said. "Who'll run the camera?"

Lars gave her a chilly smile. "I know much about machinery—of all kinds. Running the videotape could be arranged." He looked at her. "Easily."

"But you'll have the same problem. Shoot me, shoot my cameraman, and you'll be like poison to any other newspeople." Pauline Fox stared at the two terrorists. "They'll know you can't be trusted."

Lars pulled on his mask. When his face was hidden again, he spoke to Pauline. "Congratulations, Miss—no, *Ms*. Fox," he said. "You have won this time. There will be no execution. And your cameraman will be allowed to leave without harm."

Callie went limp with relief. Pauline took a

21

long, deep breath and then moved toward the exit where the cameraman would be released.

But Lars barred her way.

"Unfortunately," he said, "I cannot let you leave. You know too much."

"You mean, how many—" Pauline said.

"How *few* of them there are." Callie cut her off. Oh, Frank, were you watching? Did you get my message?

Lars nodded. "I am afraid I cannot let you go off and tell your police. You will have to join the other hostages. I will inform your cameraman." He moved toward the cockpit.

Pauline Fox stared after him, dazed. In two seconds, she had gone from neutral observer to helpless pawn.

"Down! Sit!" The newswoman was shoved into the seat across the aisle from Callie.

Pauline stared around wildly. "What? How?"

"No talking!" The terrorist's voice rose in a screech. Pauline Fox took in the gun clutched in his hand, the venomous look in his eyes—and stayed silent. The man smiled in triumph and started patrolling the aisle again.

Pauline Fox slumped limply in her chair, arms wrapped around herself as if she were warding off a chill. Her usually perfect hair was askew, and her skin was gray.

Glancing around to make sure the gunman wouldn't see or hear her, Callie whispered,

"Thanks. You saved my life. That was pretty brave."

"Brave? So were you." Pauline turned hopeless eyes toward Callie. "But I think I just traded my life for yours."

Chapter

4

FRANK HARDY SLAMMED his hand down on top of the television set. "They can't stop it there! What happened to Callie?"

R. O'Neill, the government counterterrorist expert, and Professor Hayden glanced at each other. Then O'Neill asked, "You know the girl, huh?" He tried to soften his voice. "Well, we'll know soon enough."

"She slipped a message across!" Frank told them. "There are just two guys aboard the plane. Only *two!* The cops outnumber them a hundred to one. They should be able to sneak up on them—"

He stopped as he saw the disbelieving look on the government man's face. "A message, eh, kid?" O'Neill patted Frank on the shoulder. "Good work."

"You can see it," Frank went on desperately. "Get a videotape of that interview on the plane. The close-up of Callie. I'll show you the code we used."

"Sure, kid." O'Neill patted Frank's shoulder again, then started to walk away.

Frank grabbed his arm. "You've got to listen to me!"

The government man shook himself loose. But in a smooth move, Frank grabbed the guy's arm once again and sent him tumbling to the floor.

Joe jumped and put a restraining arm out to keep Frank from doing anything else. "I don't think you convinced him," Joe whispered in his brother's ear.

"I'm sorry. I don't know what came over me," Frank said to the man.

"You little twerp!" O'Neill growled, getting back to his feet. He looked ready to deck Frank, until a hand landed on his elbow. O'Neill's glare of annoyance turned to a look of shock. "You!"

The man restraining O'Neill looked perfectly ordinary. In fact, he looked almost *too* ordinary, from his rumpled suit to his slightly scuffed shoes. But looks could be deceiving. And it was obvious that O'Neill recognized him.

The Hardys knew him only by his code name, Gray Man. He was an agent of the ultrasecret government organization called the Network, and he sometimes acted as their contact man.

"You're sure you want to draw all this attention to yourself?" the Gray Man asked.

O'Neill looked around at the gathering crowd and blanched. He quickly took off.

"Um, thanks," said Frank.

The Gray Man slowly shook his head. "Who else but you would be throwing punches in the middle of a crisis—especially at a U.S. Espionage Resources agent?"

"Espionage Resources?" Joe glanced after the government man, who had now disappeared. "But his name tag said he was with the National Advisory Committee on Terrorism."

The Gray Man rolled his eyes. "A front organization," he said. "You don't think he's going to advertise, do you?" He tapped his own name tag.

Joe read, " 'H. P. Gray, Council on International Law.' "

A dignified-looking elderly lady appeared beside him. She wore a name tag for the same organization. But the Hardys knew her real job. She was the head of the Network, running it from a mansion in Virginia. They had saved her from an assassination attempt in an adventure they called *The Lazarus Plot*.

"We're surprised to see you here, ma'am," Joe said.

"But why?" the woman asked with a dazzling smile. "I'm the honorary chairman of the Council on International Law. I have to put in an appearance, even though I detest the idea of a meeting about something as violent as terrorism.''

The Hardys saw the ironic glint in her eye.

''Well, I'm glad to see you. We've got something for the Network,'' Frank whispered. Walking to a corner, he told her about Callie's message.

The smile disappeared from the woman's face. ''There's nothing we can do about it.''

''Nothing?'' Frank repeated.

She said no more, just walked off into the crowd.

''Interagency politics,'' the Gray Man whispered. ''Our people are not supposed to get involved.''

''But what about the message?'' Frank asked. ''Can't we talk to whoever *is* running the case?''

Now it was the Gray Man's turn to give them an ironic smile. ''Would you believe U.S. Espionage Resources?'' he asked. ''You blew your chances with Roger O'Neill. He'll never listen to you now. And even if he believed you, there's nothing to be done.''

The sour look on the government man's face intensified. ''It doesn't matter if there are two men or two hundred aboard that plane. They've got guns, and innocent passengers will get killed if we try anything. Not to mention that bomb.''

The Gray Man took a deep breath. ''We don't even know that there are just two terrorists.'' He raised a hand as Frank started to protest. ''I'm sure your girlfriend *saw* two terrorists. But they may have additional people planted among the passengers, ready to leap into action *if needed.*"

He let that sink in for a moment, looking at their mutinous faces. "So do me a favor. Leave this one to the professionals." Then a glint came into his eyes. "But if I know you two, you won't butt out. So I'll do what I can to help—which won't be much." He shrugged.

"The Network can't be officially involved. Still, if we get a chance to show Espionage Resources up . . ." He grinned. "Interagency politics works both ways." He nodded a goodbye and disappeared into the crowd.

Frank smiled bitterly at his brother. "Just great. Callie risks her life to get a message out from that plane, and nobody wants to hear it—officially."

"Maybe you just didn't tell it to the right person," Joe suggested.

Frank turned to him. "You mean Dad?"

Joe nodded. "Seems worth trying."

Fenton Hardy was amused to hear about the code. "And all these years I thought you were just getting an education," he said.

But he was deadly serious when he heard about Callie's message. "Only two," he said, eyes thoughtful. "That's a help. Let's see if we can get hold of one of the house phones. There are a lot of people I'll want to call."

28

Before they could set off, however, a TV crew surrounded Fenton and the boys.

"Mr. Hardy," said the correspondent. "I'm Gil da Campo. EuroNews Syndicate. Could we take a few minutes of your time? We'd like your comments on the hostage situation."

Fenton Hardy stared at him. "There's nothing to discuss. As far as I'm aware, the situation hasn't changed."

Then he realized that the camera was already running. "What is this?"

"I understand that one of the hostages, a Miss Shaw, is a friend—a close friend—of your son." Gil da Campo extended his microphone to Frank. "How does it feel to have a loved one trapped aboard the plane?"

"What?" Frank stepped back as if the mike thrust in his face were a live snake. A cameraman with bright red hair stepped forward, focusing in.

"Gustave!" da Campo shouted. "Tight close-up!"

The Minicam operator darted around Fenton Hardy, pursuing Frank. But the Hardys were able to escape into the crowd. The EuroNews crew fell behind them. "Thank you for your comments!" da Campo called.

Fenton Hardy shook his head as he rejoined his sons. "Let's get to that phone," he said.

While their father made his calls, Frank paced back and forth, trying to work off his anger.

"You've got to hand it to these ANWO guys,"

Joe said. "They've got guts. How do you think they managed to gimmick all the TV sets in here?"

"A VCR broadcaster, like the gadget that lets us see rented films on all the sets in the house," Frank responded absently. Then he stopped in his tracks. "That's the question I should have asked," he said. "I'm really losing it."

"Well, you answered it now," Joe said. "Maybe we could track it down."

"With all the TV people around here?" Frank shook his head. "Network, local news, foreign syndicates like the one that nailed us on the floor out there." He paused. "What was it that terrorist said on the tape? That the demands would be passed on to the media."

The Hardys looked around the conference center, which was still crawling with TV crews. "What better place to give a tape to a newsman?" Joe asked.

Fenton Hardy returned. "My friends in high places thanked me for the information but don't know what to do with it. Officially, the government is still formulating policy."

"Which translates to stalling for time," Frank said.

"But they do have a new line on this Army for the New World Order," Fenton Hardy said. "It's a real lovely group. They recruit anybody, from either end of the political spectrum. The only unifying force is that they want to destroy the world as it is now. When that's done, they'll fight among themselves to decide what the new world order will be.''

''Sounds great,'' said Joe.

''Problem is, their ideas may be nutty, but their leader is brilliant.'' Fenton Hardy's face was grim. ''He's only known as the Dutchman. CIA reports have him coming from Germany. The FBI's files say he's from Holland. And Espionage Resources believes he's a South African. He'd worked for a lot of wild causes, then went free-lance, planning raids and bombings for other terrorist groups. Looks like he was raising money for his own bunch the whole time.''

''So now we have ANWO.'' Frank ran a hand through his hair. ''We just had a thought about their next move.''

Fenton Hardy nodded as he listened to the boys' suspicion that the taped demands would be passed on to one of the media people. ''I think we can ignore the small outfits and the foreign groups,'' he said. ''These guys will go for the big league.'' He smiled. ''Well, there are three network news offices here, and three of us. What do you say we each keep an eye on one of them?''

The news office was humming, everyone moving at high speed. People walked in and out, getting new film packs, batteries, and cups of coffee to recharge themselves. Frank even saw

31

some familiar faces as correspondents checked in.

But his job was boring. All he could do was keep an eye on as much as he could see. That wasn't what he wanted to do. He wanted to *move,* to *do* something to help Callie. Frank almost grinned to himself. Now I know why Joe hates stakeouts so much, he told himself.

He stifled a yawn and looked longingly at half a ham sandwich left on one of the desks. Then a man passed the desk, and Frank came alert.

Gustave, the redheaded cameraman who had chased him across the convention floor, walked into the office. He stopped by a rack of video-tapes and slipped a cassette box out of his pocket. The boxes in the rack were all black. The box in Gustave's hand was red. He slipped it into the rack, turned around, and walked out.

Frank stepped back, not wanting to be recognized. But he did notice one thing—the badge on Gustave's chest. It was a network badge, not the EuroNews tag he had worn before.

Letting Gustave get a small lead on him, Frank swung onto the cameraman's trail. He's up to something, Frank told himself. But will he be our first link to ANWO?

All of Frank's attention was on Gustave. So when he felt a hand on his shoulder, he jumped. "Cool off," a voice whispered in his ear. He turned to see Joe's grinning face.

"Saw you walking off, and you didn't look like you were heading for the john."

Frank quickly explained the situation with Gustave. "I think he's connected with ANWO. The only problem is, how do we prove it?"

Joe's grin got wider. "I've got a way." Frank's eyes continued to follow Gustave as his brother whispered in his ear. Both Hardys grinned at each other. Then Joe faded into the crowd as Frank continued tailing Gustave.

Gustave Villen slipped into a quiet stairwell, ready to disappear from the conference. He was completely unprepared when the door banged open again, hitting him in the back. He staggered forward, nearly tumbling down the stairs.

Gustave whirled around to confront the cold, furious face of the guy his crew had filmed. "I-I'm sorry about the interview, Monsieur Hardy." His voice went high with fright. "It's my job—"

"Shut up, creep." Frank Hardy had cut him off. "I know you've got some kind of connection with those guys on the plane. I'm going to find out what it is."

"I don't know what you're talking about," Gustave protested. "I'm a Belgian citizen, working for EuroNews—"

"That's no EuroNews tag on your chest," Frank said, breaking in. "I saw you sneak into that news office and plant a tape. If we play it, I

33

bet we'll find ANWO's list of demands. You're working for them. And you're going to tell me all about it, right?''

Gustave realized he couldn't deny the accusation. He didn't even try. His eyes went cold, and a gravity blade appeared in his hand.

One flick of his wrist, and the four-inch knife blade clicked into position. Then he lunged forward, giving Frank Hardy his answer—an overhand stab, aimed straight at his chest!

Chapter

5

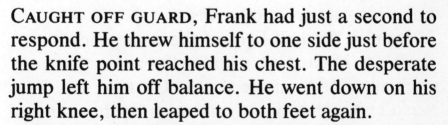

CAUGHT OFF GUARD, Frank had just a second to respond. He threw himself to one side just before the knife point reached his chest. The desperate jump left him off balance. He went down on his right knee, then leaped to both feet again.

The force of Gustave's thrust actually sent the knife into the metal door, scoring the paint. But Gustave recovered quickly and whirled around, his back to the door.

He blocked Frank's path back to the safety of the convention floor.

Gustave grinned. He had him now. If Hardy tried to head down the stairs, he'd have Gustave's knife at his undefended back all the way down. He could try to back off from Gustave and take the stairway up to the next floor. But he'd be slow moving backward—and if he turned to run,

he would again present Gustave with an undefended target.

And even if he made it to either floor, he
couldn't escape. The doors were locked. Gustave's associates had taken care to leave open
only the one stairwell door and the door to the
underground parking lot.

Full of confidence, Gustave advanced. He'd
herd this Frank Hardy back until he had him in a
corner. Then he'd silence him—permanently—
and be on his way.

Frank Hardy gave ground slowly but steadily.
From Gustave's crouch and the way he handled
his weapon, Frank could see that the Belgian
knew his way around knives.

Even in the half-light of the emergency stairs,
the blade of Gustave's knife glittered.

Frank tried to circle around Gustave, but there
wasn't enough room to maneuver on the cramped
stairwell. Gustave slashed at Frank, forcing him
back again. Then he laughed. "*Non, non,* Monsieur Hardy. You don't want to rush back to the
seminar now. Not until we have finished our little
tête-à-tête."

I'm running out of time—and room, Frank
thought. He faked left, and as Gustave moved to
block him, he jumped to the right, onto the stairs
leading up to the next floor.

Frank scrambled up the stairs, grabbing for the
handrail. Gustave charged after him, his knife at
the ready. Got to time this just right, Frank told

himself, casting a glance over his shoulder. Gustave had just gotten into the perfect position for Frank to attack. With both hands on the railing, Frank pushed off, lashing out with his left foot in a karate kick.

His heel caught Gustave right on the point of the chin.

Gustave's head snapped back, and he tumbled down to the landing below. He landed flat on his back, his arms flew out, and the knife went skittering from his nerveless grasp.

When Gustave started taking notice again, he saw Frank Hardy wedging the knife into a crack in the concrete stairs. Frank stomped down on it, snapping the blade in two.

Then he loomed over Gustave. He was still breathing heavily from the fight, and his face was red. But it was the murderous fury in his eyes that made the Belgian terrorist cringe. "Please—" he said.

"Now you're asking for favors." Frank's voice was hoarse as he looked down at Gustave.

All the fight knocked out of him, Gustave got up on his hands and knees, trying to scuttle away.

But Frank grabbed and twisted a clump of Gustave's red hair in his hand. "Now I *know* you're one of those ANWO creeps. You're working for the guys who've got my girlfriend. I'm going to find out what you know, or you're going to go flying down these stairs—headfirst."

Frank tightened his hold on Gustave's hair as

he dragged him up the stairs. "Talk—while you still can."

"Monsieur, you don't understand. They'd kill me. I—I *can't*."

"We'll find out about that," Frank said grimly. Either you start talking, or I'll fling you down this flight of stairs, then the next one, and the next—" He yanked Gustave's head back so he could look him in the eye. Frank looked angry enough to do it.

"I'll keep doing it until I run out of stairs, or until there's not enough of you left to pick up."

Frank grabbed Gustave's belt and began swinging him back and forth. Gustave's arms waved feebly as Frank prepared to push him. "Last chance, Gustave. One—two—ughh!"

Frank suddenly went limp. Gustave dropped to the stairwell floor, gibbering in French as his chin hit the concrete. But when Frank flopped down beside him, Gustave realized this was his chance to escape. Gustave started to scrabble away but instantly bumped into two heavy boots. He looked up into a pair of ice-blue eyes.

A young blond man leaned against the door to the convention floor. He rubbed his left hand over a big, competent fist. "You must be Gustave," he said.

"What—what happened?" Gustave asked.

"Quiet!" commanded the blond man. "I took care of this fellow." His English was good, but there was a faint trace of accent—German?

"There is trouble. The operation has been compromised. This man found you and other members of the army." He took a deep breath. "I must warn the Dutchman."

"Your contact—" Gustave began.

"Is now being watched!" The blond man cut him off. "The message must go through. We may have only minutes. Give me someone I can talk to. You can go, and I will warn the others." He prodded Frank Hardy's unmoving form with the toe of his boot. "I'll take care of this one, too."

Gustave licked his lips. He wasn't so eager for grand struggles right then, especially if the whole operation was going wrong. At last, he made up his mind. "The Hole-in-the-Wall—a sweet shop on Pennsylvania Avenue. Ask for Lonnie."

"And the recognition code?"

Gustave hesitated.

The blond man gave him a sharp look. "Come. There must be a recognition code!"

Gustave finally gave in. "You must say, 'The day dawned most promisingly.' And he will answer, 'Like a new world.' "

"That is all?"

Gustave nodded. "That is all."

A smile crooked the blond man's lips as he leaned over the Belgian. "Thanks, pal."

The sudden switch from an accent to pure American English made Gustave glance up in astonishment. That's how he saw the fist flashing for his jaw. Then he didn't feel astonished. He was out cold, slumped on the floor.

Frank Hardy groaned as he sat up. "What do you have in those boots, Joe, lead weights?" He rubbed his ribs. "And did you have to be so realistic?" he asked his brother.

"Steel toes," Joe answered with a grin. "I had to convince that guy, didn't I?" Joe nudged the unconscious Gustave with his foot. "What do we do about this guy?"

Frank pulled off the Belgian's belt and pulled his arms together. "Tie him up, call Dad, and be out of here by the time he comes to collect Gustave." His face was hard as he looked at his brother. "We've got a date at the Hole-in-the-Wall. With Lonnie—and maybe the Dutchman."

Chapter

6

THE HARDYS HAD some trouble finding a cab driver who was willing to go to the Hole-in-the-Wall. It was in a tough neighborhood and not very conveniently located from the conference center. It would mean a trip through heavy downtown traffic.

But if their trip was slow, it was also scenic. Their route took them along the south side of the Mall, with all the white marble museums. Then the dome of the Capitol Building rose up on the side, and the cab cut over onto Pennsylvania Avenue.

Government buildings began to thin out then. Once they were past the Library of Congress, Pennsylvania Avenue started changing. Neighborhood-type stores began appearing. And the farther they traveled, the more run-down the neighborhood became.

"This is the street the president lives on?" Joe asked.

"Well, not on this end of it." The driver grinned. He began to make another joke when the radio cut in with a new report on the hostage situation.

"A videotaped set of demands from the Army for the New World Order has been discovered in a major network news office," the announcer said. "The leader of the group has explained that there will be no negotiations. Four members of his group presently in prison in France must be released, U.S. antiterrorist advisors must be withdrawn from foreign countries, and a million-dollar ransom is to be delivered to the plane."

"Those guys are sure doing a number on us," commented the driver.

But Frank was leaning forward in his seat, straining to hear the rest of the report.

"These demands must be met within the next twelve hours," the announcer went on, "or, according to the tape, the International Airways jet—and everyone aboard—will be blown up."

Frank and Joe looked at each other. "Twelve hours to find this guy," Joe muttered.

"Are we getting near that address we gave you?" Frank asked.

"Next corner," the driver responded.

They looked down a row of shabby storefronts,

some of them boarded up. On the corner was the candy store they wanted. Its side and front windows had been crudely filled in with cement blocks and the whole front given a quick once-over with white paint, now gone dingy.

A crudely hand-lettered sign stood over the door.

HOLE-IN-THE-WALL

CANDY, SODAS

Joe gazed from the sign to the store. "Great name. Describes the place perfectly."

"At least the door is open," Frank said. "Somebody must be in there. Let's go."

They stepped through the doorway and went from bright Washington sunlight into gloom. Whoever owned the place didn't believe in a lot of light. With the windows blocked up, the two forty-watt bulbs hanging from the ceiling didn't begin to light up the store.

It smelled of dust and sweat. Frank squinted his eyes, making out a counter by the entrance and a soda fountain along one wall. "Hello?" he called.

"How do?" As Frank's eyes got accustomed to the dimness, he realized a man was sitting on one of the fountain stools. He did his best not to stare as the man labored toward them on a cane.

The man topped Frank's six-foot-one height

43

and was incredibly heavy. Billows of fat rolled over the waist of the man's worn jeans and rippled under his torn undershirt. Tufts of white chest hair peeped out, too.

Joe glanced at his brother, his thoughts evident in his eyes. Samples too much of his own candy.

But as the man stepped into the light from the front door, both Hardys gasped. The man's right arm and half of his face were a mass of scar tissue.

The man's lips curled into a smile as he looked into their faces. "Got this courtesy of the U-nited States Marine Corps. Was in a demolitions unit. But one of the timers was screwed up. Dang near demolished *me*."

He leaned on his cane. "They retired me, and I had enough money to get me this nice store. So what can I get for you gentlemen? A candy bar? A nice lime rickey?" With his heavy southern accent, those last words sounded more like "lahm rickay."

"We are looking for Lonnie." Joe did his foreign-English routine again, pronouncing every word very carefully, as if he had to think about it.

"I'm Lonnie. A couple of foreign boys, hey? Sure you wouldn't like some soda pop?"

"No. We came in to get out of the sun." Joe fanned himself with his hand. "The day dawned most promisingly."

Lonnie's eyes suddenly became sharp. "Like

a new world," he responded. "So. I see you boys need something more than soda." He waddled past them, closing the door. "Come in the back." Joe and Frank followed him, nearly choking in the stench of stale sweat.

Lonnie led them into a combination office and storeroom, piled high with crates. Joe leaned against one that had just been pried open and glanced inside. "Heckler and Koch machine guns," he commented.

"I can still use my old Marine contacts to get guns for the cause," Lonnie said, settling his bulk behind a desk. "Still got some buddies. Even down in the barracks by the Navy Yard. And, of course, there are my demolition skills. I built the bomb that's in the airplane."

He leaned back, and suddenly an old Army Colt automatic appeared in his hand. "I also know all the people who would use that recognition code—and you're not any of them."

"Gustave sent us," Frank said, imitating Joe's accent. "He fears the airport operation has been compromised. People are after him."

"So he sent you?" Lonnie asked.

"There is more," Joe said. "But we are to report only to the leader." He hesitated for a second. "The Dutchman."

Lonnie frowned. "That's not standard procedure. The Dutchman operates only through cut-outs."

Frank nodded in understanding. Of course he

would use cutouts—innocent-looking go-betweens—to receive his reports and issue his orders. It made sense that ANWO's leader wouldn't run the risk of being traced through direct contact with his agents.

"Why don't you pass the report on to me?" Lonnie said. "I'll pass it straight to the big man."

"You are so close to the leader?" Joe asked.

"Don't let this dump fool you, sonny." Although he still held the pistol on them, Frank noticed that Lonnie's grip had relaxed a bit. "I got this store because it's a perfect contact spot. There's even a disco around the corner where lots of foreign students hang out." He grinned. "Seems real natural that some of them might stop off for a soda or such."

"A good cover," Frank said. "But this report cannot go in the usual way." Frank had to choose his words carefully. This guy was obviously one of the higher-ups in ANWO. "The report is for the leader's ears alone. The leak comes from too high a level."

Lonnie's frown got worse, but he put down his gun. "It's Beauvoir, isn't it? He wants us to fail—even get captured—so he can take over." He shook his head. "I warned against letting him into this." He looked at the Hardys. "Am I right?"

"I cannot say," Joe responded, in just the right voice to confirm Lonnie's suspicions. In a group as crazy as this, there have to be lots of factions, he thought. Let him blame whoever he likes.

Lonnie leaned back in his chair. "I'm right, aren't I? Can't put much over on me. I been on the drill here more years than you been around." He leaned farther back, looking reminiscent.

"Our message," Frank pressed, not really wanting to hear about twenty years of wacko politics.

"I been thinking on it," Lonnie said. "Don't know where the Dutchman is, myself. But Pia sure will. A good kid, Pia. And an easy contact for you kids. Just go up to Georgetown. I'll give you the number where you can reach—"

He reached over for a pad and pencil. But just as he put pencil to paper, the sound of sirens came screaming up the street. "Sounds like a whole convoy of cop cars," Lonnie said, pausing.

"A familiar sound in this area, I expect," said Joe.

But as the sirens got louder and louder, Lonnie's face became more thoughtful. Frank risked one glance at the gun. Could he beat Lonnie to it?

Lonnie surprised him. He leaned back again in his chair, way back, resting his hand on an old fuse box behind his desk.

"You know," Lonnie said, "I sure as sugar hope you're not snitches or undercover cops."

The Hardys could barely hear his voice over the noise of the sirens outside.

47

" 'Cause I decided a long time ago I wasn't going to get caught." Lonnie gave them a lop-sided smile as he looked down at his half-crippled bulk. "And I sure can't run."

He swung open the door of the fuse box. It was crammed with what looked like yellowish clay. "CN—plastic explosive." Lonnie flicked a big black electrical switch in the middle of the bomb. "And this switch here activates a detonator."

Lonnie rose to his feet. "Now, if anybody's fool enough to open the front door, we're all going to go up like the Fourth of July."

Chapter

7

FRANK AND JOE both charged for the fuse box, but Lonnie stood in the way.

Joe threw a whistling right, straight into Lonnie's gut. His fist penetrated four inches of blubber, then hit rock-hard muscle.

"Hunh!" Lonnie grunted. Then his massive fist caught Joe in the side of the head, sending him spinning away.

Frank tried a karate blow to Lonnie's neck. But again, Lonnie's fat cushioned the blow.

He picked Frank up with both hands and threw him across the office. Frank crashed into the wall and slumped to the floor.

Ears ringing, he forced himself to his feet. The office was quiet now; the sirens had stopped blaring. Any second, someone would be coming through that door.

Frank's eyes fell on the old pistol still sitting on the desk. He lunged for it, almost had his fingers around the butt—

Then he dropped it as Lonnie lashed into his shoulder with his cane.

"No way, boy. If we're going to go, we're going to go."

Joe came staggering up for another attack, sidestepping Lonnie to get at the switch. He managed to get his fingers into the box, only to have Lonnie's cane rammed into his stomach. Joe folded in pain. All he had to show for it was a sticky coating of CN on his fingers.

Frank stopped rubbing his injured shoulder and grabbed left-handed for the gun. Lonnie's cane swept out, sending the pistol spinning away.

But the grab had been only a feint. While Lonnie was distracted, Frank's right hand had crept painfully into his pocket. It came out with a small spray can.

As Lonnie brought his cane around again, Frank brought his hand up. His aim was pretty shaky, but the spray did its job. It jetted into Lonnie's face.

Lonnie screamed, his cane falling to the floor as he brought both hands up to his eyes.

Frank lurched past him, his own eyes tearing as he passed through the cloud of liquid tear gas. He flicked the switch to the "off" position. Please, don't let it be booby-trapped, he prayed.

Nothing happened. They didn't blow up.

50

But Lonnie did. With a roar, he started flailing his arms around. Even blind, he was a formidable opponent. One of his hamlike fists caught Frank a glancing blow, knocking him to the ground. The little can rolled from Frank's hand.

Lonnie fumbled around the fuse box, trying to rearm his bomb.

Then Joe hit him in a flying tackle. They both disappeared behind the desk as Lonnie lost his balance and hit the floor thunderously.

Frank got to his knees and found the pistol resting on the floor beside him. Picking it up, he started for the desk. "Joe? You okay?"

"Yeah." Joe reappeared, grinning and brushing dust off himself. "I was lucky. He didn't land on me." He picked up the aerosol can and looked at it curiously. "What is this stuff?"

"Mace," Frank said. "Something else I bought at the—"

"Freeze!" bellowed a voice from the doorway.

Frank turned to find three policemen braced for a fight, their pistols all aimed at him.

"Drop the gun!" one of the cops ordered.

Frank opened his hand. The heavy Colt thudded to the floor.

"All secure," the policeman reported. They parted, and Roger O'Neill, the agent from U.S. Espionage Resources, entered the room. He gave the Hardys a disgusted look. "I don't believe it," he said. Then he called over his shoulder, "You've got to see this."

Fenton Hardy appeared in the doorway. He didn't look disgusted. Concerned, yes. Upset. And as the boys looked into his eyes, they realized "angry" might be the best description.

"Um, hi, Dad," said Joe.

"I don't know what to say." Fenton Hardy shook his head, disappointed. "I thought we were supposed to be working *together,* staking out those news offices. Next thing I know, you call me about that Gustave fellow and disappear. We interrogated him, you know. He told me everything—" He began to look angrier. *"Everything."*

"Yeah," O'Neill said. "We know how you've been playing junior detective."

Meanwhile, the policemen had found Lonnie and handcuffed him. O'Neill waved them off impatiently as they approached Frank and Joe.

Frank tried to explain things to his father. "We had to do something. For Callie. She's trapped on that plane."

"I understand that," Fenton Hardy said. "But you're not going to save her alone. Don't you think the U.S. government might help?"

Joe gave O'Neill a sideways glance. "They haven't been much help up to now," he muttered.

"Boys, I trusted you, and look what's happened."

Frank's head came up. "Two ANWO agents caught. We've gotten the first break in this case." He glanced over at Agent O'Neill. "While the

52

older and wiser heads were doing nothing." His eyes locked pleadingly with his father's. "We've heard that ANWO has set a twelve-hour deadline for their demands. They'll blow Callie up—"

Fenton Hardy turned away. "There are one hundred and fourteen lives at stake here, *besides* Callie Shaw. And your reckless behavior has endangered them all." He sighed. "Agent O'Neill has requested—demanded—that you stop impeding his investigation. He's escorting you to the airport to put you on the first plane back to New York. Then straight on to Bayport. Understand? I'll stay on—"

"Dad," Frank said, interrupting, his voice low. "If Mom were on that hijacked plane, what would you do?"

For a long moment, Fenton Hardy didn't answer. Finally, he said, "I-I'd go along with the government." But they all heard the quaver in his voice.

Agent O'Neill cut in quickly. "Come on, kids, I've got a car for you." He led them out of the office. Fenton Hardy didn't turn around.

Outside, the whole neighborhood was crawling with uniformed police, carrying rifles and shotguns.

"Let's clear the way here!" O'Neill shouted, waving his government identification. The cops parted before the magic ID, opening a lane to the big black sedan surrounded by police cruisers. Two men in dark suits and sunglasses got out of the car. They popped to attention when they saw their superior.

"We're taking these kids to the airport," O'Neill told his associates. "Peterson, you're responsible for getting them on a plane to New York. In fact, you'll fly with them, to make sure they get there." He gave the Hardys a nasty smile. "That way, we won't have any more surprises out of you."

Peterson opened the rear door, and O'Neill waved the Hardys in. Frank slid across the seat and touched the handle on the far door, with a vague idea of opening it and making a getaway.

O'Neill seemed to read his mind. "Go on, try it." There seemed to be no lock button, but when Frank pulled on the handle, it didn't give.

"This is a company car," O'Neill explained. "If you want the back doors to open, the driver has to press a button up front." He nodded to the driver. "Try it now."

The door opened, but Peterson stood ready to block any escape.

"Now, stop thinking up silly stunts like that, and let's get going."

Joe got into the car, then O'Neill joined the two brothers in back. Peterson sat with the driver in the front.

O'Neill's ID was as effective at clearing away cop cars as it had been at clearing away cops.

Frank and Joe sat in silence as the car retraced

the route they had taken to reach the Hole-in-the-Wall.

O'Neill had Peterson busy on the mobile telephone, checking out flights to New York. "We're in luck," he reported. "There's one with seats available, and we should be there fifteen minutes before departure." He gave the Hardys another sour smile. "I'll be glad to have you two out of my hair, even if it means a delay in interrogating that guy we caught in the candy store."

Frank looked at the government man, then stared out the window. Obviously, O'Neill was never going to forgive Frank for throwing him in the middle of the convention floor.

"Of course, he may have told you kids something." O'Neill made the comment very offhandedly, studying his fingernails. "Sooo"—O'Neill drew out the word—"if you have anything to tell me, it had better be now."

He looked at Frank. Frank glanced at Joe.

"You mean, like secrets and stuff?" Joe said. He managed to make himself sound like a little kid.

A flash of irritation appeared in O'Neill's eyes, but he managed to keep his temper. "Yeah, something like that."

"Gosh, no," Frank chirped in. "He was a seasoned terrorist. He'd never give secrets away to a couple of kids."

O'Neill had had it. "Okay, you two," he snarled. "I see you'll smart-mouth me right to

55

the end. But if I find out you impeded a federal investigation—''

"Me?" Joe said, the voice of injured innocence.

"Us?" said Frank, his eyes wide.

O'Neill bit back the retort he was about to make. He crossed his arms and settled back in his seat.

It was at that moment that a taxi rammed into the back of their car. O'Neill lurched forward, just managing to get his hands up to brace himself against the front seat.

He reached into his pocket for his ID card. "He rammed into the wrong car this time!" O'Neill pulled on the door handle. Of course, it didn't open. "Hey, Peterson, open this up. I'm going to talk to this guy."

Peterson obediently leaned over and hit a button on the console. Frank and Joe glanced at each other. As O'Neill opened his door, Frank operated the handle on his side.

He waited till O'Neill was nose to nose with the cabbie, then pushed against the door. It swung open, and they dashed out into the street.

Chapter

8

Traffic heading for the Potomac bridges was heavy. Frank and Joe almost got run over twice before O'Neill realized they were escaping.

"Hold it!" he yelled.

Frank had to grin at how easily they had gotten away, but the grin disappeared when he saw Peterson starting to run after them. At least he had to dodge traffic, too, so Frank and Joe had a respectable lead on him.

"How are we going to lose him?" Joe asked, on the sidewalk now.

"I have no idea!" Frank responded.

They ran for a couple of blocks, with Peterson closing the gap. Dodging through the homebound office workers, Joe glanced over his shoulder. "Still there," he puffed.

Frank was starting to gasp for breath, too. He

had a stitch in his side, and the shoulder that Lonnie had clobbered was beginning to throb. But Peterson was still getting closer.

How do they train those guys? Frank wondered.

They plowed on, Peterson still gaining. Escape plans ran through Frank's mind. Maybe they could duck into an office building, go out a side exit, and lose him. But what if there weren't any side exits? They'd be trapped. And Frank didn't know the buildings around there.

Other half-formed schemes floated around in his mind, but nothing really solidified. Frank began to get worried. He could usually come up with *some* sort of plan.

Just ahead of him, Joe turned and waved his arm. "This way!" He plunged through an entrance and down an escalator. Frank followed his brother in a broken-field run down the moving steps. Then he knew where they were heading— into a station for the Metro, Washington's subway system.

Frank brightened. Grabbing a train would be the perfect way to lose Peterson. Of course, they'd have to buck the ticket lines. Unless— Frank shrugged. They were already on the run from the government. What difference would it make if they beat the fares?

He followed Joe straight to the turnstiles. But Joe didn't take a running jump. Instead, he dug out his wallet and produced a small card.

When Frank saw the computerized plastic strip on the side, he recognized it as a Metro fare card! Where had Joe gotten it?

Now wasn't the time to ask. Joe slipped the card into a sensing device, and the turnstile barrier swung open. Then he flung the card back.

Frank snatched the card in midair, then inserted it. As he ran through the turnstile, he could see Peterson charging up. The government agent was groping in his jacket. Frank went pale. He couldn't be thinking of shooting—not in this crowded space!

But no, no one was that crazy. Peterson whipped out his own fare card. Frank didn't watch him, though. His attention was on the blinking lights on one of the platforms. That meant an incoming train!

Behind him, he heard a wild yell. Frank turned to see Peterson tumbling to the ground. He had tripped over a commuter's feet. Frank didn't get a good look at the commuter—he was wearing a gray suit. Could it be? No. The Gray Man couldn't have tailed them.

Frank joined Joe in the crush on another escalator, heading for the train that was pulling in. They rushed for the doors, managed to squeeze in. The doors hissed closed, just as Peterson reached them.

He was still pounding on the doors as the train pulled out.

Joe grinned at Frank. "Lucky I had that old ticket, huh?"

"Where did you get it?" Frank wanted to know.

"A souvenir, I guess you could call it. Last time I was down here, I used one of those automated machines to get a fare card. You know—you slip a bill in, push buttons to show how much money goes on the card, and get change."

Joe shrugged. "I put a five in the machine, but it wouldn't give me any change. So I wound up with five dollars on my card. I didn't use it up, so I held on to it. No machine gets away with cheating me!"

Frank smiled. "So, when you saw the Metro entrance you knew we could get on."

"Yeah," said Joe. "The problem is, where do we get off?"

"Three stops," Frank said, squinting at the system map. "Then we change trains."

"To throw Peterson off our trail?"

Frank nodded. "And to head for our next contact."

Joe looked puzzled and opened his mouth to speak. Then he looked at all the ears around them and shut his mouth.

A short time later, the Hardys rode an escalator up to the surface again. "Dupont Circle," Frank said. "This is about as close as the Metro comes to where we're going."

"Which brings up a question. Where *are* we going?" Joe asked. He followed Frank around a huge traffic circle, then down a block of turn-of-the-century houses. "Pretty nice," he said, looking around. "But we've gone two blocks, and you haven't answered my question yet."

He sighed. "We managed to get away, but we've got no weapons—unless you count the plastic explosive I wiped off onto my handkerchief. They even took away the can of Mace. We're going up against a bunch of terrorists with machine guns. To top everything off, we're going in blind. We didn't have time to get anything out of Lonnie. We don't know who to see or where to find this Dutchman."

"If we get the Dutchman, we'll have a hostage ANWO can't ignore," Frank answered. "And Lonnie *did* tell us about his contact." He grinned. "First of all, Lonnie gave us a name—Pia. A girl's name."

Joe stared.

"Remember?" Frank said. "Lonnie said he couldn't help us. We had to see Pia. And we'd have to go to Georgetown. He was just about to give us her number when he heard the sirens."

"So, we've got a name and a neighborhood—but a pretty big neighborhood. What do you plan on doing, walking the streets and calling her name?"

Frank smiled. "I'm hoping to cut it down a little bit," he said. "There were two other things

Lonnie said. First, he called Pia a good kid. So I guess she'd be young.''

"Okay. What was the other thing?"

"Lonnie said it would be an easy contact for us. 'You kids.' Those were his exact words.''

"So?" said Joe.

"So where in Georgetown would you find a lot of kids?" asked Frank. He grinned at Joe's growing understanding. "Right. The university.''

Joe shook his head. "So we've got to check out a whole school.''

Frank clapped Joe on the back. "And if there's a man who can find one girl in a thousand, it's Joe Hardy,'' he said.

They stopped off at a used-book store to buy props so they'd look like students, then walked the rest of the way to the university. Nobody bothered them as they found their way to the cafeteria. A few minutes later, Joe was chatting with a cute blond.

"Hey, Maddie, I can't believe how lucky I was to meet you,'' he said. "Think you can help me set up my friend here?'' He gestured toward Frank, who sat at the far side of their table, looking off into the crowd.

"I don't know,'' Maddie said. "He looks cute enough.''

"He's into causes. Any girls around here like that?''

Maddie shrugged. "I don't know. That's not really my crowd.''

"He's heard about a girl he really wants to meet. Her name is Pia."

"Oh, *her*." Maddie's nose wrinkled. "Crazy Pia." She looked at Frank again. "Funny. He doesn't look weird."

"Weird?" Joe looked puzzled.

"Well, why would he be interested in somebody like Pia? I mean, she's really crazy. Always talking like the end of the world is coming. She's the Queen of Weird!"

"Do you know where he could find her? He really wants to meet her."

Maddie turned to give Frank a long, disbelieving stare, while Frank concentrated hard on looking as weird as possible.

Finally, Maddie shrugged. "I never see her in classes. Nobody ever does. But I suppose she's in the Student Union. She's usually there, painting signs for weird causes."

Joe stood up. "Maybe I'll take my friend to go meet her."

Maddie shrugged again. "Go ahead. But no way am I going to double with her." She grinned and nodded at Frank. "With him, maybe. But not with her."

Frank pretended not to hear, but the color rose in his face. Callie was in horrible danger, and this girl was trying to flirt with him.

He turned to Maddie and gave her his gooniest smile. "Did I just hear you say you'd like to go out with me? They're having a march to ban

63

chrome on cars. It'll help us save precious natural resources. Maybe you'd like—''

"Um, I don't think I could make it," Maddie said quickly. "But this girl I know, Pia, would probably love to go. I just told your friend here where you could find her."

"Great!" said Frank. "If you change your mind—''

"I don't think so," Maddie said. To Joe, she whispered, "You aren't like that, are you?"

"Oh no," Joe whispered back. "I *like* chrome on cars. See you later." He waved goodbye to Maddie. All the way out of the cafeteria, he had to fight a wild urge to break into laughter.

"Chrome on cars?" he muttered as they walked to the Student Union. "You smooth-talking devil, you!"

The Student Union was a big underground complex, with lots of places for a sign painter to hang out. Joe and Frank spent a lot of time looking but got nowhere.

While they talked to one kid who was tuning his guitar, a campus security guard walked by. The Hardys tensed for a second, but the guard walked right past them.

"I'm looking for Olympia Morrison," the guard said in a loud voice. "Anybody know where she is?"

"Pia?" One girl pushed back her hair and pointed. "She's over in the corner, painting."

Joe and Frank both followed her arm. There,

in the corner, a girl dressed all in black sat with some pieces of posterboard, painting what looked like slogans.

She stopped as she became aware of people looking at her. Then she saw the guard. In one fluid movement, she was up and running.

"Hey, wait!" called the guard. He took a couple of steps forward. But Pia only ran faster.

"Hey!"

"What's going on?" The kids in the room were all looking around now.

The guard just shrugged. "I don't know." He tapped a note in his hand. "The dean just told me to deliver this to her."

But Frank and Joe hardly paid any attention. They were pushing their way through the crowd, already in hot pursuit.

Chapter

9

Tracking Pia Morrison wasn't easy. For one thing, she had a lead on the Hardys as she left the student union and darted across the campus. For another, it was Friday evening, and the streets of Georgetown were beginning to fill.

"Where did all these people come from?" Joe muttered as more and more people clogged the streets. In seconds he passed some students, two guys in suits with briefcases, a family of tourists, and eight suburban teenagers obviously looking for action.

One of the teenagers jostled Joe back, shouting, "Hey, watch where you're going!" He hooked Joe's arm, swinging him around.

Pia moved like a running back through the opponent's defensive line, zipping easily through momentary openings in the crowds.

66

Things weren't so easy for the Hardys. They were bigger, so their efforts to make a path usually earned them dirty looks from jostled pedestrians.

Frank's chest tightened as he watched his one hope for saving Callie slip away. His frustration mounted as Pia disappeared into the crowd. He wanted to slam his way through that uncaring herd and catch that girl.

Save it for the bad guys, Frank told himself. Desperately, he rose up on his toes to scan the jammed sidewalk. Then he saw her—Pia was crossing the street. "Come on!"

Crossing in the middle of the block wasn't easy. The traffic was bumper to bumper. But Frank and Joe finally found a space they could squeeze through, and then they had to work their way through the crowd on the opposite sidewalk.

It was slow torture, pushing against the mob. Everyone seemed to be ambling, looking in the windows of the shops along the street. And, of course, the local hangouts had heavy foot traffic in front of them, too. Everything had slowed to a crawl.

The Hardys finally reached the corner and glanced around. Pia wasn't in the crowd. Finally, Frank noticed a dark figure legging it down a side street. "There!"

Off the main drag, they made better time. Joe held out an arm to stop Frank from charging headlong. "Better not make too much noise," he said. "We don't want her turning around to see people running after her."

They moved at a jog, keeping Pia in sight and slowly drawing closer. She led them through a beautiful neighborhood, with rows of old colonial townhouses. The sidewalks were made of blocks of slate, old-fashioned and uneven—perfect for tripping a running pursuer.

After three blocks, Pia turned a corner. Frank and Joe broke into a cautious run. They reached the cross street and saw Pia enter a townhouse in the middle of the block.

A moment later, they were standing in front of the house. Three buzzers stood by the door, one for each floor of the building. The middle one read, "O. Morrison."

Joe whistled. "Pretty nice for a plain college student," he said.

"Maybe Daddy's paying for it," Frank suggested. His voice grew grim. "Or maybe ANWO." He jabbed at Pia's button. "She ought to be upstairs by now. Get ready with your magic accent."

A frightened voice came over the intercom system. "Yes?"

"You are Pia, yes?" said Joe, sounding equally nervous. "You do not know us. But we have a message. You must help us."

Seconds ticked slowly by until the voice on the other side finally said, "A-all right. Come up."

The buzzer sounded, and they headed up the

stairs. A door on the second floor swung open, and Pia stood outlined in the light, checking them out. Frank noticed that she kept her right hand out of sight behind the door frame.

As they came level with her, the Hardys finally got their first good look at Pia. She was slender—skinny, really. The black jeans and sweatshirt she wore hung on her, emphasizing rather than hiding her skinniness.

Her dark hair was stringy, and her face fell just short of pretty—a little too pinched to be attractive. Right then, with her lower lip between her teeth, she looked like a scared rabbit. Round glasses magnified her pale eyes.

"S-stay right there," she said as they reached the landing. Now her hand came into view. It was holding a small Beretta, and even though the muzzle was shaking, it was close enough to hit one of them. "Now. What are you doing here? You said something about a message."

"From Mr. Lonnie," Joe said. "I am Josef. This is Franz." Frank nodded. "Mr. Lonnie, he was . . . recruiting us." Joe paused for a second, as if trying to think of the right word. "For the New Order. He gave us your name in case anything went wrong."

Joe shook his head. "I think something has. We went to his store—you know, the Hole-in-the-Wall? And there were policemen all around it. I think they were arresting Mr. Lonnie. Franz and

I, we did not wait to see. We thought you should know this.''

Pia's eyes went round with shock. "First Gustave, now Lonnie. This is bad.'' Then she abruptly became businesslike, tossing the pistol onto a table by the door. "We'll just have to add their freedom to our demands. Come in. I'll have to decide on our next move.'' She closed the door behind them.

An open suitcase sat in the middle of the living room, with piles of clothes, papers, and books around it.

"You can see I was getting ready to leave,'' Pia said. "One of the school cops came to get me today. I think someone may be on to me.''

Joe almost opened his mouth to say the guy was just bringing a message, then shut it. He wasn't supposed to know that. He just nodded, marveling at Pia's paranoid life-style.

"I was going to go to the safe house, where we were supposed to meet after the operation. But now—'' Pia shook her head. "I don't think so. Lonnie knew about it.''

Her rabbitlike teeth started gnawing at her lower lip again. "I know he'd die rather than give away a secret, but we can't be sure. They could use truth drugs on him.'' She motioned to Joe to go to the window. "We've got a front view of the street. You keep watch. I've got to get ready.''

"We will do everything we can to help you,'' Joe promised.

Pia threw aside most of the clothes and the books. The papers she tossed into the old-fashioned fireplace, setting a match to them. "We'll have to travel light," she said. "There's an important stop we have to make. He'll need my report to change the plan." She coughed. "Someone I need to see." She glanced at them, her newfound trust faltering for a second.

Frank's heart began to pound. That "someone" she was talking about could only be the Dutchman.

"Can we go with you?" he asked. "Josef and I, we are afraid. What if Mr. Lonnie talks about us? We are not yet members of your army, but I hope you will help us."

"Don't worry," Pia replied, all confidence again. "If Lonnie recruited you, that's good enough for me. We take care of our own. I'll make sure of it. After all, you brought us this warning—"

"Pia! Look!" Joe stood by the side of the window so he could keep an eye on the darkening street without being seen himself. Pia and Frank rushed over to peek out.

The street below them was suddenly filled. A long black car, surrounded by police vehicles, pulled up. All of the officers moved out silently.

"A surprise raid," Frank said. His brain slipped into high gear. He recognized O'Neill's customized car. That meant Lonnie had talked. O'Neill—and maybe Fenton Hardy—would soon be bursting through the door. Once again, he and Joe would be shipped off to Bayport—this time under armed guard. If they were lucky, they might make Pia tell them where the Dutchman was. But even if the government captured the ANWO leader, his release would probably wind up at the top of the terrorists' demands.

Would the government really keep the Dutchman in prison and let a planeload of people die? Frank didn't think so. There had to be a better way.

He made up his mind. "Is there another way out?"

Pia nodded. "Right. Come on."

She forgot to pick up her pistol. She even left the papers burning merrily in the fireplace. Frank and Joe followed her into the bedroom, where she started throwing shoes and junk out of her closet.

"I don't—" Frank began as Pia got down on her hands and knees on the closet floor. Then he shut up as he watched her slide out a panel in the back wall. "This will take us into the closet of an apartment in the next building," she explained. "We'll be coming out a block away."

Pia eased her way into the crawl space, followed by Frank and Joe.

I sure hope nobody's home, Frank thought.

As if she were reading his mind, Pia told them, "The apartment is empty. It's rented by one of our people, but he never uses it."

72

She eased open the closet door on the other side, and they emerged into darkness. Pia headed for the apartment door, but Frank slipped over to the window. "Wait," he whispered as she prepared to open the door. "Look here."

They stared into the street below. It, too, was crawling with cops. "I guess they figured we might go over the roof or something," Pia said. "They must have surrounded the whole block."

"Trapped." Joe breathed out loud.

"No," said Pia. "We still have a way out."

She led them down the stairs to the ground floor, then down another flight to the basement. "Careful," she whispered. "It's old. The ceiling's very low."

"Ah," said Frank, nearly braining himself on a ceiling beam.

Pia fumbled at a shelf, striking a match. Then she lit a candle stub, which threw a wan circle of light. "At least we can see where we're going now."

Half bent over, she led them deeper into the cellar. "We're under the sidewalk now," she said. "You can hear some of the footsteps."

Listening carefully, the Hardys could indeed hear noises above them.

Pia led them forward until they faced what seemed to be a blank wall. She counted bricks from one corner, then slammed her hand against one.

With the faintest squeal, the center of the wall

began to pivot. "It's more than a century old," Pia said. "Before the Civil War, this was an Underground Railroad escape tunnel for runaway slaves. It goes under the street, through the graveyard, and into another basement. They'll never be looking for us there."

Pia took some keys and money from her bag. These she pocketed and then led the way with her candle, crouching down as she stepped into the musty tunnel. The air smelled as if it hadn't been breathed for at least a hundred years.

The tunnel started out as a bricked vault, but as they went farther along, it changed. The ceiling started to slope, until finally they had to crawl. Then the brick disappeared altogether, leaving them in a dirt tunnel with infrequent wooden support beams.

Maybe this is the part under the graveyard, Frank thought. He had no idea how far they had come. He just followed the dim circle of light that was Pia's candle.

Suddenly, Pia stopped. Frank nearly ran into her. "There's a tricky part here," she said. "One of the beams has fallen in."

Great, Frank thought as she worked her way around the fallen wood. "Did you hear?" he called back to Joe. "A fallen beam."

Joe tapped Frank on the ankle, letting him know he understood.

Then it was Frank's turn to squirm through the half-blocked opening. He eased his shoulders

74

through, careful not to touch the wood. This won't be easy for Joe, he thought.

When he was almost through, Frank heard a noise just above his head. Must be under the street again. That sounds like a truck up there.

There was no time for thought as the truck jarred to a stop—and the roof of the tunnel thundered down on Frank!

Chapter
10

THE TUNNEL ROOF didn't fall on Joe. Instead, darkness hit him—a terrible darkness, so deep he could see nothing. One moment he was groping along after Frank, and then came that complete blackness.

He rubbed his eyes, coughing on invisible dust. So this is what it's like to be blind, he thought.

"Frank? Pia?" he called. Maybe Pia had dropped the candle. She looked like the flaky type to him.

No answer.

"Guys?" Stretching his arms forward, he tried to feel his way. Inches from his face, he hit loose earth. A cave-in.

Joe fumbled around, making sure the whole tunnel had been filled. It had. It looked as if he'd have to turn back.

But as he groped around along the tunnel floor, he found something that froze him. A shoe. Frank's shoe. And as he felt farther, he realized a foot was still in it. Frank was trapped under the dirt!

Desperate, Joe tapped against Frank's ankle. He got an answering twitch. Frank was alive!

Joe began clawing at the cave-in. Frank might be alive, but there was no way he could breathe under all that dirt.

Hurling the loose earth behind him, Joe worked to free his brother's legs. He uncovered a piece of wooden bracing and used that as a shovel. Now he was up to Frank's waist. Joe dug frantically. At least the roof still held. No more dirt came cascading down.

As he felt himself being freed, Frank began to wriggle around. Joe got the message. He got a hold on his brother and pulled.

Frank came free unexpectedly. The two of them tumbled back in the darkness, both coughing in the dust.

"Are you okay?" Joe finally managed to say.

"Yeah." Frank's voice was hoarse but strong. "I was lucky. When the dirt came down, I wound up with my head between my arms. That left a little air pocket around my face. Otherwise—"

Otherwise, you'd be breathing dirt, Joe thought. "Well, you're out now. The question is, what do we do?"

"Well, I don't see us going forward," Frank said.

"I don't see *anything!*" Joe gave a short, bitter laugh.

"The problem is, if we go back, we'll be walking into the arms of the cops."

"*And* Dad, and O'Neill. They'll have us on a plane so fast—"

"I guess that means we go forward," Frank said.

Joe fumbled around. "Well, there's a piece of wood around here somewhere."

They set to work digging through the obstruction before them.

"Hold it!" Frank said. "I think I heard something."

Joe paused, and they both heard a scraping noise coming from the far side of the cave-in.

"That must be Pia working toward us," Frank said. "Come on!"

They dug quickly, fearful that another truck would come rumbling over them and undo all their work. The noise had sounded pretty close. Maybe the cave-in wasn't that big.

Then Joe's piece of wood rammed into something coming from the other side—a piece of wood in Pia's hands. "Franz? Josef?" Her voice was shrill with terror. "My candle is out! I can't see!"

For a second, Frank almost forgot his false identity. He remembered just in time to put on his fake accent. "We are here," he said, taking Pia's hand while Joe enlarged the hole. "Right here!"

As soon as the hole was large enough, Frank and Joe crawled through to a more stable section of tunnel. Pia's voice quavered. "I thought you were buried."

"Just a little," Frank said. "I am all right."

Then Pia shook herself, as if to make her fear go away. "We must be almost at the other end. Follow me."

And soon enough, the bottom of the tunnel turned to brick under their knees again. After that, they came to a dead end. Frank and Joe both leaned against the walls of the tunnel as Pia fumbled for the release in the darkness.

Then they heard a rusty squeal as a section of wall pivoted. Pia fumbled around again, this time outside the tunnel. A line of light appeared at the edge of the doorway. All three of them blinked, raising their hands. Even the dim basement bulbs were blinding after their trip through darkness. Joe thought he'd never seen anything that looked so good as that basement.

Frank staggered out into the basement, staring around at the boxes and plastic bags that filled the space. "What is all this?" he asked.

"Clothes," Pia answered. "We're in the basement of a boutique. Our cause owns the building and rents it out. The store makes a good cover." She stopped short, then burst out laughing as

Frank turned around. "Oh, Franz!" she said. "Just look at you!"

Every inch of Frank was stained with dirt. His clothes, his hair, his face—he was even leaving dusty footprints wherever he went. But he began to laugh as he looked at Pia and Joe in the light. They weren't much better off.

"Well, you are lucky, Pia," he finally said. "You can get new clothes. But for me—" He held up a sequined minidress. "I do not think so, do you?"

"You're right. This is a women's shop. But I suppose there's something here I can change into," Pia said.

She disappeared around a rack of clothes to try on her choices. Joe and Frank attempted to beat some of the dust out of their own clothes, but it was a pretty hopeless job. Frank wondered if the dirt on his hands and face was permanently ingrained.

"Well, what do you think?" Pia asked as she stepped back to join the boys.

"Ah," said Frank. Pia had worked hard to change her appearance. She wore a checked shirt and a pair of tailored jeans. Even her hair was different, combed back and pulled into a bun. Except for her glasses, she looked like a different girl. Almost pretty.

"Nice," Joe said. "Very nice."

Pia actually blushed. "I don't usually dress this

way," she explained. "But I thought to fool the
police—"

"Oh yes," Frank agreed. "I would be fooled."

Pia blushed some more. "I think we should be
moving. The police won't be looking for us on
the other side of the graveyard. But it's not a
good idea to hang around."

She led the way up the stairs, pausing cau-
tiously at the top step. "I'm going to turn the
light off, just in case," she said, hitting the
switch. Then she slowly eased the door open and
peeked around. "As I said, closed. Nobody's
here."

They stepped out into the darkened shop. Pia
went to the door, peering through the glass. "I
don't see anyone outside," she reported. "No
police."

Pia rattled keys in the locks. "That'll do it,"
she said. "We can step out of here, free and
clear."

She swung the door open. A piercing siren
went off.

Pia froze. "What?"

"They gave you all the keys," Frank said.
"They did not mention the new alarm system."

He grabbed Pia's arm and bolted from the door.

"This will draw them," Joe said as he followed
them.

"Draw?" Pia echoed.

"The police. With all of them around, many
will answer this call," Frank explained.

As if to underline what he said, they heard the not-too-distant sound of sirens.

"Have to get out of here," Frank said as they rushed along the tree-lined streets. "Do you have any ideas?"

Pia shook her head. "We have nowhere else in the neighborhood."

Frank scowled. "No place to hide. Can we get back to the crowds?"

Again, Pia shook her head. "Wisconsin and M streets are behind us. The police are blocking our way."

"We may as well stop running. It will only call attention to ourselves."

They slowed their pace to a fast walk. Joe kept glancing over his shoulder. But so far there were no signs of pursuit.

"For once," he said, "luck is on our side. Maybe we—"

At that moment, a police cruiser turned the corner three blocks ahead of them. Then it was coming straight at them, slowly, its searchlight playing on both sides of the street.

Chapter

11

FRANK AND JOE stared at each other in panic. They had only seconds to come up with a plan. "Back—into those bushes," Joe hissed. Frank didn't even hesitate. He slipped into the shadows.

As the car approached, Joe folded the astonished Pia in his arms, turning her away from the street. He slipped off her glasses and, as the police car came up, started kissing her. They stood that way for a long moment, until the searchlight caught them. Pia jumped away, half-blind and blinking, the picture of surprise.

A policeman leaned out the car window, trying to hide a smile. "Sorry to bother you, kids. Someone tried to break into a store a couple of blocks back. We're looking for them. Did anyone come running past you?"

Pia shrank back in fear. But to the policeman

she just looked embarrassed. Joe was left to answer the question. "Uh, well, I didn't see—I mean, I don't think so," he said. "Um, I didn't notice—"

The policeman's grin grew broader as he listened to Joe's fumbling explanation.

"Stop digging yourself in any deeper, kid. I guess you didn't see anything."

"I-I thought I saw someone passing," Pia said timidly. "I didn't really look. It could have been a man or a woman. But they were heading in that direction." She pointed back the way the police car had come.

The policeman nodded. "Thanks. We'll get some units over there. And, kids, why don't you use Lover's Lane?"

They could hear the cop's laughter as the car started off down the street. But through the window Joe could see that he was already talking on the radio.

"What have you done?" he asked in a furious whisper. "The police are already behind us. Now they will be searching ahead of us as well."

"I-I thought they would turn around and go away," Pia stammered.

"Your thinking was not right," Joe muttered. "As you saw."

"They are gone?" Frank asked.

Joe looked down into the shadows. With his stained face, Frank was completely camouflaged.

He grinned at his brother. "I think pretty fast, no?" he asked.

"That reminds me," Pia said. She shook Joe's hand. "That's for saving us, Josef." Then she gave Joe a ringing slap across the face. "And *that's* for trying something like that without asking me."

Joe rubbed his cheek, while Frank tried his best not to laugh.

"There's no time for this." Pia quickly slipped her glasses back on. "We have to get out of here."

"But where?" Frank asked. "Police to the east, police to the west."

"We go north," Pia said. She hesitated. "I have a friend who lives up that way."

Frank kept a careful poker face, in spite of his excitement. He remembered Pia's slip earlier. Her "friend" had the power to change ANWO's plans. It had to be the Dutchman. But why would the brains behind the hijacking have such an obviously inexperienced contact?

Actually, it made a strange sort of sense. Who would pay much attention to a radical-cause groupie? Pia made the perfect cutout for the Dutchman. And, with luck, she would lead the Hardys to her boss.

They set off along the streets, taking a zigzag route. Sometimes they even circled around blocks. Frank gave Pia a look. "Are you trying to confuse us?" he asked.

She shook her head. "It's standard procedure. To make sure no one is following us."

Joe shook his head. "If anyone was following, we'd already be arrested."

Pia shrugged but continued with her strange route. Several times, they saw police cars in the distance. None of them ever came close.

After leading them in a circle around the Naval Observatory, Pia looked over her shoulder, still checking to make sure they weren't being followed. "Good," she said. "Everything's okay. Now we head down Massachusetts Avenue, across the bridge, and out of Georgetown."

They were three blocks from the Massachusetts Avenue Bridge when they saw the roadblock.

It was discreet, a couple of police cars off at the side of the road. But it was clear that the cops were checking everyone who crossed that bridge.

"Over," said Pia, turning abruptly. "We'll try the Buffalo Bridge on Q Street." They walked a block and turned onto Q Street.

The cops were waiting there, too.

Pia stood very still, staring at the collection of police cars. "They'll be covering every bridge back into the city, won't they?" Pia whispered.

"Looks like it," Joe agreed.

Frank began thinking furiously. "These bridges," he said, "they go over a park as well as Rock Creek."

"Rock Creek Park," Pia said.

Frank remembered crossing the M Street Bridge, farther south. It cut across a ravine with a creek below. "There was an *autobahn*—how do you say? A freeway down there, too," he said. "We must get over that."

"What are you saying?" Joe asked.

"We go into the park, climb down to the creek, and cross it," said Frank.

Pia nodded eagerly. "We should try it under the P Street Bridge," she said. "Someone told me that Washington's army crossed the creek there, marching down to Yorktown."

"Good," said Frank. "First we must get into the park."

Getting in wasn't too difficult—a quick climb over a fence. Getting down to the creek *was* tough. The ravine walls were steep and heavily overgrown. And the darkness didn't help.

"Can't even see where I'm going," Joe muttered in his brother's ear. "This stupid— whoooah!" He slipped on a rock and tore through some bushes.

By the time they finally reached the creek, each of them had a good collection of scratches and scrapes.

"There is the freeway. On the other side of the water," said Frank, scouting out the territory.

"Yeah. There's the bridge where it crosses over the creek. So we can follow the creek under the freeway and cross the creek itself." Pia patted him on the shoulder. "Good thinking, Franz."

Frank grunted noncommittally. "After we cross the water, then I will be happy."

"At least there are no police," said Joe.

"No sense in waiting." Pia turned to the Hardys. "Let's go."

All three slipped off their shoes and hung them over their necks. Their socks went into their pockets, and they rolled up the legs of their pants.

"Careful," said Frank. "Watch your feet."

They edged into the water. Pia winced. "Cold." She shivered.

Frank just grit his teeth and kept moving.

The water was soon up to their knees and slowly crept higher the farther they moved. Even with their jeans rolled, it was obvious that they were going to get soaking wet.

They continued to slosh their way through to the far side. Then, after pausing for a while to let their soggy clothes dry a bit, they put their shoes back on.

"We're aiming for Sheridan Circle," Pia said. "Maybe we can walk beside the freeway and then climb up."

Frank and Joe just shrugged. The climb down hadn't been fun. Somehow, they suspected a climb up would be even worse.

Pia led the way through the underbrush, guiding herself by the gleam of headlights on the freeway nearby. Finally, they reached the grassy margin of the freeway.

"Just a couple of blocks now," Pia said.

"How high up?" asked Joe. "We still must climb the ravine."

"It's worth it," Frank whispered. "At the end of it, we meet the Dutchman. And when we get him . . ."

The brothers caught up with Pia, who had suddenly stopped. Then they saw why.

Parked by the side of the road was a car—a large black car. It looked horribly familiar. So did the man leaning against the fender—their old friend, Roger O'Neill.

They could see the look on his face in the intermittent beams from headlights—the smile they had seen before.

"Well, well, well," O'Neill said, crossing his arms. "Now, why did I expect to see you here?"

Chapter

12

FRANK AND JOE glanced at each other. How had O'Neill followed them? He must have known about the tunnel. And when the cop reported seeing the kids near the store, he could have added it up and tailed them.

But no more time to wonder; in about three seconds, O'Neill would open his mouth. Pia would find out that they weren't Franz and Josef, and she'd never lead them to the Dutchman. Even if she informed on her leader, considering O'Neill's track record, he'd lose the guy. Or worse, he would blow the plan.

There was only one thing to do. Frank stepped forward. "I do not understand, sir." He looked pleadingly, desperately, into O'Neill's eyes. "We were just walking."

O'Neill leaned back on the fender. His nasty

smile only grew larger. "Yeah. Through the water. Stop giving me this innocent act. I've got you, dead."

He drew himself up, reaching under his jacket for his gun. "You are under—"

"Schwein!" Joe burst out. If he was going down the tubes, he decided to go down in character.

O'Neill jerked out his .38 Special. "You little creep!" He swung the pistol up and caught Joe on the side of the head. Joe crumpled to the ground. O'Neill brought the gun around for another blow.

Frank had no choice. He launched off on his right foot, his left foot sweeping up. The high kick caught O'Neill in the forearm, swinging the gun off course.

Twisting around, O'Neill aimed at Frank. But Joe threw himself at the government man's knees. They both went down in a heap, O'Neill clubbing Joe again.

Frank jumped forward, and O'Neill revealed his own martial-arts training. He launched a snap kick at Frank's head. This wasn't a blow meant to stun. It could injure, even kill.

Frank barely saw the foot coming at the side of his head. But O'Neill's timing was off. There was the briefest hesitation in his attack, and that saved Frank's life.

He scrambled desperately away, and O'Neill's heavy shoe just grazed his ear. Frank jumped back. As O'Neill regained his feet, the gun came up again, and this time Joe was in no shape to help. Frank tried a desperation play, his right leg sweeping around in a circle to catch O'Neill behind the knees.

The government man toppled to the ground. Frank swung him around, one arm immobilizing O'Neill's gun hand. His fingers reached for the pressure points in the neck. Seconds later, the agent sagged, unconscious.

Frank felt no triumph. If he had had troubles before, he had major ones now. Breaking and entering—or, rather, exiting—and now attacking a federal officer. If Frank couldn't free the hostages after all this, he'd probably be better off flying away with the hijackers.

Pia bustled in and frisked the unconscious government man, digging out his wallet. While she withdrew to examine the papers, Joe came over from the car, carrying a couple of pairs of handcuffs. "We're in luck," he whispered. "The car's empty."

Frank shook his head again. "I'm still not thinking straight. It never even occurred to me to look."

Joe grinned. "I think I know why he didn't want Peterson or his driver around. Looks like O'Neill wanted all the glory for capturing us."

"Well, I don't know how this will look on his record." Frank jerked O'Neill's wrists behind his back and cuffed them. He used the other pair of handcuffs on the government man's ankles.

"Help me get him in the car," he whispered to Joe. "Then we've got to get out of here."

"Right," said Joe. "Somebody is sure to report your roadside karate demonstration."

As the Hardys tucked the government man into the backseat of the car, Pia reappeared with O'Neill's ID in one hand and his gun in the other.

"U.S. Espionage Resources," she said flatly, bringing up the gun. "He deserves to die."

"No time," Frank said quickly, smacking the barrel with the flat of his hand, forcing it down. "We must get out of here. And a shot will make more people remember us."

He took out his handkerchief and wrapped it around the pistol, taking it from Pia. "No fingerprints," he said. Then he took the wallet. "And no identification."

Winding up, he flung both gun and wallet far off into the underbrush. "Now, we climb."

The ascent up the other side of the ravine was a nightmare. Now gravity was against them, and they were already tired. They were covered with sweat by the time they reached the top. Frank's face showed thin streaks of white where the sweat had cleaned away some of the ground-in dirt.

Just as they reached the top, the scream of police sirens cut the air. They looked down to see three cruisers pull up beside the black car.

"You were right," Pia told Frank. "We had to get out of there."

"And now we must get out of here," Frank said, agreeing. "Where do we go?"

"We're almost there," Pia said. "Follow me."

She led the way out of the park, cutting around a large house. "The Turkish Embassy," she said. "Good. Here's Sheridan Circle."

They stepped onto the street and saw a large open space before them. In the center was a bronze statue—the Civil War general Sheridan on his horse, leaning back and swinging his cap as if to rally his troops.

"Which way?" asked Joe.

"Around the general," Pia answered with a grin. She seemed very sure of herself as she led them past houses—more like mansions—around the circle. Frank saw lots of brass plaques.

"This is the south end of Embassy Row," Pia explained as they passed the buildings. "Romania, Ireland, Guatemala, Cyprus—"

"All next door to one another," Joe whispered. Frank gave him a look, telling him to knock off the commentary.

"The house we're heading for isn't quite so large," Pia explained. "But it is connected to one of the embassies." Her eyes became guarded once again. "The person we're going to see has powerful friends."

I'll bet, thought Frank, wondering which country was willing to help the Dutchman in America.

He had no time for other thoughts. Pia had darted down another street and stopped in front of a house that didn't look like a mansion—at least, not a *very* rich mansion.

She ran right up to the front door and pressed the bell. Even though the windows were dark, the door was opened immediately—as if she were expected.

Standing framed in the oversize doorway was a short, pudgy man in a sweater too large for him. His forehead was high, fringed with thinning blond hair. He had fat round cheeks, like Santa Claus, but they weren't a healthy pink. They were pale, sallow. almost yellowish. He had the look of a man who spent too much time indoors.

Quickly, he beckoned them in, then shut the door. His lips were curled in a smile, but jowls sagged at the sides of his face, pulling the smile down. His nose was short, and his glasses slid to the tip of it. His chin was weak, too small for the cheeks and jowls.

But his eyes were sharp, a sparkling blue. They darted from Pia to the Hardys as he laughed. "Ah, Pia, my poor, poor dear. You look as though you've been playing in the mud." He glanced again at Frank and Joe. "And who have you been playing with?"

"Franz, Josef," she said, "meet—Karl."

Those sharp eyes took in Frank and Joe again. "Franz? Josef?" He started speaking to them

95

rapidly in a guttural language. German? Dutch? Frank couldn't tell.

Pia touched his sleeve, looking hurt. "I don't understand what you're saying. And didn't we agree? All members of the cause will speak English."

"Ah," said Karl. "But I did not know I was speaking to members of the cause." His eyes narrowed behind his heavy lenses. "Which is strange. I thought I knew everyone in the cause."

Frank kept his face carefully blank, hiding his excitement. They must be very close to the Dutchman now. This guy would have to be a special lieutenant. Maybe the guy they were looking for was right in this house!

"Lonnie had just recruited them," Pia explained.

"Lonnie is under arrest." Karl sounded as if he were having just an ordinary conversation, but both Frank and Joe noticed that his right hand had not left the pocket of his sweater. They knew he had a gun in there.

"I know," said Pia. "They came and warned me. Otherwise, I'd have been arrested, too!" She raised her arms, showing off her bedraggled state. "Why do you think we look like this? We've been on the run!"

Karl's hand almost came out of his pocket. "You were followed here?" His accent became much stronger all of a sudden.

Pia shook her head. "We gave them the slip.

96

But we had to wade across Rock Creek. And on the other side, a government agent was waiting! Franz took him out." She smiled and gave Frank an admiring gaze. In fact, Frank realized with embarrassment, it was more than admiring.

"He knocked the guy out and left him tied up in his car. Then we came here." Pia turned all business again, looking at Karl. "I think we've finally found just the people we need for the reinforcement action."

Karl smiled. "I believe you may be right," he said to Pia. His right hand finally came out of his pocket—empty. He rubbed it against his other hand with a dry, rasping sound. "But you must think I am a terrible host. Please wash up, and I will get you something to drink. Then we will discuss business, yes?"

Frank left the bathroom feeling one hundred percent better. His clothes were still damp from the trip across the creek, but at least he was clean. He had managed to remove all the dirt from his face.

He followed the scent of brewed coffee into the kitchen. It was a large room, with a huge, round oak table in the middle. Frank's stomach rumbled when he saw a silver tray piled high with thick sandwiches. Beside it were cans of soda and cups for coffee.

But the wooden chairs around the table were empty. Frank stood by one of them, hesitating.

Should he try to find the others? He sat down. Joe could take care of himself. And he wanted a look at the papers piled beside the tray.

He spread out a wide, rolled-up piece of paper and gasped. It was a plan of the airport. Marked in red was the area around Gate 61. The outline of an airliner had been inked in there. The International Airways jet!

Also on the map were arrows and notes in blue. They seemed to lead back to one of the hangars.

"Look at him!" A voice cut through Frank's puzzled thoughts. "He takes so long, I have to give a tour of the house to entertain you. Then he sneaks into the kitchen. But does he look at the food? No! He looks at the papers!"

Karl laughed heartily as he led Pia and Joe into the kitchen. "So? Do you like my plans? I worked very hard on them, I assure you."

Frank stared up in astonishment. Karl's last three words rang in his head. The same words— the same voice—as the faceless figure on the videotape. Frank couldn't believe it. *This* was the mysterious Dutchman? This pudgy little account-ant type? Somehow, Frank had expected some-one more polished, more sinister—more *young*. He dropped the papers and stared.

But the Dutchman stared in equal surprise when he saw Frank cleaned up.

"You aren't a Franz," the Dutchman rasped. "You're a Frank! Frank Hardy. I saw the tape that Gustave shot on television! You have a girl on the plane.''

He straight-armed Joe, sending him staggering against the table. Then he whipped out a Walther pistol from his sweater pocket. ''You may have found your way here, but you'll never leave. Not alive!''

Chapter

13

THE SHOCK OF having his cover blown might have stunned even a professional into a fatal paralysis. But Frank Hardy was moving even as Karl brought his gun up. He kicked his chair away and dropped under the table as flame flashed from the muzzle of the Walther. A bullet whistled through the space where he'd been sitting an instant before.

Frank hit the floor. "Missed me—Dutchman."

Hearing his professional name shocked Karl into a second's hesitation. But he could afford it. He was holding a gun with twenty shots against a boy with no weapon at all.

Yet it was the unarmed boy who used that hesitation to launch an attack. Bracing his feet under the edge of the big kitchen table, Frank heaved, making the whole table tilt. Then it fell over with a crash, bouncing on the floor, scattering food and drink all over the kitchen.

The Dutchman jumped back in alarm, squeezing off a shot into the falling table. A nine-millimeter bullet tore through the oak of the tabletop. It passed over Frank's head. Close, but not close enough. Karl couldn't see where to aim.

He never got a chance for another try.

Frank pivoted around, using the table itself as his weapon. He shoved his shoulder into the tabletop and wrapped his arm around its pedestal. Joe had also dropped to the floor and behind the tabletop. He realized what Frank was up to and reached over to give him a hand. Together, they launched the table like a giant battering ram.

The Dutchman had lost the advantage. He was waving his gun, trying to decide where to shoot, when the table seemed to attack him. It caught him head-on, smashed into him, and sent him sprawling backward.

Karl hit the floor hard, arms and legs flailing. The gun left his hand, skittering across the shiny kitchen floor like a stone skipped across a lake.

But Frank hadn't finished yet. Rising to his feet, he braced himself and kicked the table again. The tabletop flew over and landed on the horrified Karl. He had time only to scream a few curses. His hands had automatically shot up to brace against the weight. He wasn't hurt, but he was trapped for a few precious moments.

Frank went to get the Walther, but it had skidded to a stop in front of Pia, who stood frozen in the doorway. She snapped out of her daze, crouched, and picked up the gun.

Events had moved too fast for her. The pistol wavered in her hand, as if she didn't quite know where to point it.

Gambling, Frank took a step toward her, reaching out with his hand. "Come on, Pia, give me the gun."

"No!" The word came like an explosion from the trapped Dutchman. He grunted, trying to shove the table off himself. "Shoot. Kill them both. Then we leave."

Blinking in astonishment, Pia still hesitated. She was obviously having a hard time thinking of Franz and Josef, the allies who had warned her and helped in her escape from the police, as enemies.

Frank took another step. He was almost within grabbing range.

But Pia finally made up her mind. Her slack face tightened up, and she swung the gun to cover him. "You tricked me!" she cried, her voice a shrill scream. "You pretended to be helping me, but all the time you were using me to get to Karl."

Frank stood still, just a little too far from the gun to try anything.

"You were working with the police all along,

weren't you? Pretending to be recruits to the cause." She glared across the room at Joe. "I thought you were so smart, tricking those cops in Georgetown. But it wasn't so hard, was it? The same way it wasn't so hard for you to beat that Espionage Resources man by the freeway."

Her lips skinned back from her teeth in a snarl. "It was good acting. But I bet he lay right down for you. I'm only sorry now I *didn't* shoot him. That would have surprised him. But no, you stopped me. Of course you would, if you were working together."

It almost made Frank laugh. Pia thought the whole horrible journey had been a setup. If only she knew!

But Pia went on, her voice growing shriller. "When I think that I worried about you when that tunnel caved in, when you fought—you made me *like* you!" She almost spat the word out. "And all the time you had another girl." If she had had a crush on him before, it was all over then. She was working herself into a fury—a murderous fury.

"Pia!" The Dutchman had finally wormed his way out from under the table. Sitting up, he glared at her, ignoring Joe. He knew he was safe. Joe couldn't make a move before Pia shot him.

But the Dutchman also wanted the gun in *his* hands. He got to his feet and walked to Pia, being careful not to get in her line of fire. "I will take care of these two. Give me the gun."

For a second, Pia looked rebellious. But all Karl had to do was repeat her name again, more sternly. He was, after all, the leader. And she was his follower. He edged forward, confidently extending his hand.

That was when Joe grabbed the full can of soda lying on the floor and threw it at the back of the terrorist's head.

The Dutchman went down like dead weight. Pia stared for an instant, then turned her gun on Joe.

Frank leaped forward, his hand sweeping down like a blade.

The gun went off, but it was pointing at the floor. The recoil and Frank's blow jarred the pistol from Pia's hand. It clattered to the floor.

But Pia wasn't finished. With a howl, she dropped to the floor, scrambling for the gun. Frank tried to grab her, but she twisted free. Pia's elbow caught him in the side of the head—not hard enough to knock him out, but enough to slow him down.

She stretched desperately, snatching up the gun. Still shaky, Frank jumped on her, pinning the wrist of her gun hand to the floor. She flailed under him, her free hand smacking against him, one knee thumping against his ribs.

But Frank wasn't about to be distracted. His fingers were clamping on the pressure points in her neck. She managed one convulsive shudder before she sagged back, unconscious.

Frank scooped up the pistol, then stood up. "She'll be in dreamland for a few minutes at least—time enough to find something to tie her up with. How is our friend Karl?"

"He'll wake up with a good-sized bump on the back of his head, but that's about it," said Joe, carefully examining the unconscious terrorist leader. "Hard to believe he's the big cheese. Somehow I kept expecting more muscles."

Frank shook his head. "When you have brains, you don't need muscles. You just recruit young, strong, desperate people to follow your plans. If they go wrong, the recruits die. So what? They are expendable."

His fists clenched. "Lots of innocent people die, too—the ones who happen to be walking past when a bomb explodes, those trapped on the airplanes that get hijacked . . ."

Joe nodded grimly. "And if a plan goes well, slugs like Karl step out from the shadows and become heroes of the movement—whatever the movement happens to be." He looked down at the Dutchman. "Well, *we've* got him now. The question is, what do we do with him?"

Half an hour later, the captives were lying tied up on the living-room floor. Joe had robbed the stereo system of wire to bind their wrists and ankles. He had also found some rags to gag them with.

Pia came to first. They could hear her make faint, muffled noises, almost drowned out by the sound of a transistor radio. Then the Dutchman opened his eyes, glaring at them silently.

Frank got up from the couch and turned the radio off. "We've been listening to the news. The same reports, over and over again. Nothing's changed at the airport." He sat down again, spreading out the papers he had retrieved from the kitchen. The plans hadn't gone through the fight unscathed. There were mayonnaise stains, a big blotch where the coffee had spilled, and a bullet hole in one corner.

Joe had been more interested in finding an undamaged sandwich than looking at the plans. Frank had only nibbled on his sandwich as he read.

For about the fifth time, Joe got up and checked the street outside. Frank didn't even look up. "If anybody had heard shots, the cops would have been here by now." He grinned, rattling the papers. "Nobody else is coming to visit. Our friend here left strict orders. No contact while the operation went down."

He walked over to the Dutchman, knelt, and loosened his gag. "You left that order, didn't you?"

"Even the best plans go wrong." He sounded like a college professor commenting on a disappointing experiment.

"This changes nothing, you know," he continued in that same calm voice. "We've already accomplished our major objective—disrupting the counterterrorism seminar. The ransom would be useful, but it is not important. And the prisoners we wanted freed . . ." He shrugged. "They are not really part of our organization. That was merely misdirection. I was much more interested in getting your antiterrorism experts out of Europe. Too much cooperation between countries would hamper my cause."

"But if your main target was the seminar, why seize the plane?" Joe demanded. "Why not attack the conference rooms, where your enemies really are?"

The Dutchman smiled. "You are very direct, my young friend. There are other ways to destroy an enemy. Instead of making martyrs of the men at the seminar, I hurt them far worse by making them seem ineffectual under the cameras of your own media. A true victory."

"Victory!" said Joe. "You're lying on the floor, tied up. Reinforcements can never reach the plane to relieve the hijackers. And you're acting as if you've won!"

"I *have* won," the Dutchman said, still calm. "My people on the plane will continue to carry out my plan—without reinforcements. Of course, when they don't appear, Lars and Habib will become nervous. I cannot be responsible for their actions in that heightened state."

Frank turned away abruptly. The Dutchman laughed.

"I know that your father is a detective—an ex-policeman. You play by the *rules*." He made the word sound like a joke.

"Oh yeah," Joe burst out. "You guys don't have to worry about rules. You just kill off anybody who gets in your way. Even if they don't get in your way. What do they say? 'Kill one, frighten a hundred'?" The muscles on his jaw stood out.

"So, you can't do anything to me, can you?" The Dutchman mocked him. "If you do, you'll be no better than I."

Frank swooped down and silenced him with the gag. "Don't push your luck," he warned.

"I don't know why we're wasting our time listening to this creep," said Joe. "We ought to be *doing* something. I mean, I don't want to get you upset or anything, but Callie is still stuck on that plane. And time is running out." He glanced over at the Dutchman. "I figure we'll pack him into a car and head for the airport—"

"Where the cops will take him off our hands as soon as we reach the outside gates." Frank finished for Joe grimly. "And then the negotiators will negotiate, and the terrorists will demand that our side set him free. Because if we don't, they'll kill all the people on the plane."

The Dutchman's eyes changed as he listened

to them. Frank suspected that if they took the gag off, he'd be laughing.

Standing over his captive, Frank looked at his brother. "You know," he said, "maybe he has a point. If we want to save those people, we'll have to forget the rules."

He spread out the plans of the airport. "The red lines and notes show his plan for taking over the jetliner. He really did it with only two guys. Nobody else is hiding on the plane."

Then he pointed to the blue lines and notes. "And here is his plan to get reinforcements aboard. In a little while, the guys on the plane are going to demand a van full of food. And these notes outline how to sneak into the airport and take over that van."

Frank glanced at his watch. "We've got time, but we should start getting ready. There are supplies—guns and stuff—hidden here in the house for this run. But there are some preparations we'll have to make that *aren't* noted down here." He smiled grimly. "For instance, that little souvenir you got from Lonnie—the handful of CN—will come in handy."

He started writing a list on a piece of paper. "Here are the supplies we'll need. I saw car keys on a rack in the kitchen. There's probably a car in the garage. Try to find an all-night store and get what we need. I'll stay and keep our host company."

Joe jumped to his feet. "At last I get some action!" he said.

Frank smiled. "And I have a plan. Or should I say"—he glanced over at the beet-red Dutchman—"*he* has a plan."

Chapter

14

CALLIE SHAW GLANCED at her watch—hours since the terrorists had taken over the plane. For about the four-hundredth time, she tried to close her eyes and rest. And once again, it didn't work. She sighed and wished she hadn't. The air in the plane was so thick, it was like trying to inhale molasses. *Hot* molasses.

With the air-conditioning off, the inside of the jet had quickly heated up. Even now, at night, the interior of the plane had not cooled off. Washington's hot spring weather had made things just about unbearable.

Callie normally would have hated the idea of fainting. But she began to yearn for the chance to faint so she could escape. She glanced around the plane. Some of the older people were really looking bad.

Pauline Fox's TV look was melting away across the aisle from her. Her hairdo had turned into individual limp strands, and all her makeup had sweated off. She just looked tired, terrified, and worn out—she looked like everybody else on the plane.

The two hijackers were feeling the heat as well. Even the icy Lars was beginning to wilt. He had taken off his jacket and tie. Habib had his shirt unbuttoned all the way down the front, and his shirttails were hanging out of his pants.

Once an hour, the hijackers had been allowing the flight attendants to serve water, one row at a time. They had also allowed people to go to the rest rooms, one every fifteen minutes. Otherwise, no one was allowed into the aisle—on pain of death.

Pauline Fox had filled Callie in on what had happened in the outside world up to the time of her own capture, whispering in short bursts while Lars and Habib weren't near. Callie had found it especially interesting that the hijackers had made no effort to deal with police or government negotiators. And certainly in the time that followed, Lars and Habib hadn't done any negotiating.

"If anything is going on," she had whispered, "it's not being handled from here. Somebody outside must be cutting the deals."

But as the hours dragged on, Callie found it harder and harder to think of a world outside the plane. Her universe had shrunk to a seat, the heat, the damp, and the odors. If Lars and Habib start shooting, they may be doing us a favor, she found herself thinking.

Finally, Lars made an announcement. "We have been here a long time, and I know you are hungry and thirsty. When we took over this aircraft, I told the attendants to turn off the ovens that heat the meals." He paused for a moment to give them an icy smile. "We did not need more heat."

Callie had to agree with that.

"Now we will ask the negotiators outside for food—sandwiches and cold drinks."

Involuntarily, the captives let loose a heartfelt "Ahh."

Lars looked almost human as he smiled again. "Soon a van will come with these items. I will ask for them now. Habib will guard you." His smile disappeared. "I need not remind you to remain quietly in your seats."

He certainly didn't have to remind them of what would happen if they didn't. Habib stood in the back of the cabin, his machine gun ready.

Lars pulled his mask over his head and went outside to negotiate for food. He returned looking very pleased with himself. "The food will be here within the hour."

Now that they had something to look forward to, all of them were sneaking peeks at their wristwatches. But the time moved so slowly that Callie soon grew bored.

Anyway, she was far more interested in the reactions of the hijackers. They were excited. Habib especially seemed to glance at his watch constantly.

Callie began to wonder. These guys aren't charged up about getting a ham sandwich and a root beer. Something else is going on here.

She looked over at Pauline Fox, who had also come alive in her seat. The newswoman was very interested, too. But when Callie looked at her and raised her eyebrows, Pauline could only answer with a shrug.

As snack time approached, Callie found herself getting more and more nervous. The terrorists were doing something nice for their captives. Why were they acting so out of character? Callie was convinced that whatever would happen, it would probably be bad. Not that she'd be able to do anything about it, though. The hijackers would be able to spread poison on every sandwich, and she wouldn't be able to get up and stop them. Or maybe she would. Dying from a bullet would at least be faster.

Then she was rudely shaken from her thoughts by Habib, who was walking down the aisle with a big bag, stopping at every seat. "We be nice to you, you help us. Money. Jewelry. You put it all in the bag, please."

Please. He walks down the aisle with a bag in one hand and a gun in the other, and he says please.

The man by the window in Callie's row dug out his wallet, pulling out a fat wad of bills. He passed them to the woman next to him, who took bills out of her purse, slipped off a gold ring, and handed the pile to Callie.

Reaching into her own pocket, Callie pulled out the money she had brought along. It wasn't much—she had left most of her money with Mr. Hardy. She had planned to hit the shops in Georgetown.

"That's all?" Habib said.

Callie nodded.

Habib pointed with his gun at the man. "You have a gold watch."

The man's face turned the color of dough as he quickly stripped the watch off. His hand trembled as he passed it over.

Then Habib looked critically at Callie. "Nice chain," he said.

Callie fingered the silver filigree chain she was wearing. Frank had given it to her when they had started going out. She wore it every day. It had cost Frank good money, but she knew it really wasn't very valuable. For a second, Callie thought of arguing. But she looked at Habib's gun and the bag he was shaking impatiently.

She sighed and started to slip it over her head.

"Achh," growled Habib. He grabbed the chain and yanked it off her throat, breaking it. He shoved it into the bag and went on to the next seat.

Callie stared after him, fingering the welt at her neck. If I get the chance, I'll make him pay for that, she promised herself.

"Stop. They're coming." Lars's voice was actually showing emotion. Why was he getting so excited over a food delivery?

Lars went into the first-class cabin, positioning himself to cover the door. Habib covered the passengers again.

They could hear the sound of footsteps coming up the access ladder.

"We bring tidings of the new day!" a voice called up.

"Then hurry the dawn!" Lars called back.

Callie blinked. A recognition code? Her heart chilled. The deliverymen must be reinforcements for the terrorists! How had they gotten past all the cops and guards outside?

Two men in gray coveralls came in, bent under the weight of a huge box.

"You heard? They knew the code!" Lars's face split in a big smile.

"Comrades! Brothers!" cried Habib.

The two newcomers put down the box, opening it. Then they stood, with machine guns of their own in their hands. "Yeah, right," said the blond-haired one, who turned to face Habib.

Callie froze in her seat. It was Joe Hardy!

Chapter

15

FRANK HARDY HOPED that the smile on his face didn't look as phony as it felt. Every muscle in his body was strained to the bursting point. He kept one hand in his pocket, clutching his secret weapon.

"You brought more weapons and ammunition?" asked Lars.

Frank nodded to the blond terrorist.

"Any food?" asked Habib.

"Everything," said Frank.

"We think you'll especially like this. It's a surprise." Joe Hardy stood by the box of supplies and reached deep inside. He hauled up the Dutchman, bound and gagged, with an assembly of electronic equipment strapped to his chest.

The whole plane became silent as the two terrorists gawked at their leader, stunned to see him brought so low.

Lars turned to face Frank Hardy. His face was at its most dangerous—totally devoid of emotion. But his eyes glittered with menace, and his fingers were white around the grip of his Uzi. "Your government has made a great mistake," he said.

"Oh, we're not government guys," Frank admitted cheerfully. "This is a strictly free-lance job."

"Even more foolish." The muzzle of Lars's gun inched up.

Frank didn't move his gun. Instead, he just held out his fist. Barely visible was a small remote-control device, about the size of a disposable cigarette lighter. Frank's thumb was over a small stud at the top.

"I hear you guys know all about bombs," he said. "So I guess you'll know a detonator when you see one. But maybe you haven't looked at your boss too carefully. You ought to check out the jewelry he's wearing."

Lars and Frank locked eyes. "Do it," Frank suggested. "Before you do something stupid."

Silently, Lars walked over to the Dutchman. The head terrorist had been bound so that he had absolutely no freedom of movement. Each of his wrists was securely bound to one of his thighs. Strapped to his chest was a mass of electronics hardware. Wires led up to his mouth. Dribbling from his lips was just the faintest trace of grayish yellow plasticine. . . .

Lars's eyes went wide.

"You *do* recognize it, don't you?" Frank asked. "Yes, it's CN. Used to belong to your friend Lonnie. He showed us his getaway bomb—before we took him down. We saved a little bit, though. Enough, say, to blow a man's head off."

Frank and Lars locked gazes again, both their faces grim. "Don't kid yourself," Frank said softly. "If I have to, I'll push the button."

Lars stepped away from the Dutchman, his face slowly going pale with the realization of what the Hardys had done. "And you call us terrorists," he whispered.

"Actually, *he* was the one who gave us the idea," Frank said, nodding at the Dutchman. "He said we'd never beat you by following the rules. So we decided to take a page from your book—where anything is allowed."

"Yeah," said Joe. "You've got everybody aboard this plane sitting on top of a bomb. So don't go complaining because we didn't treat your boss with kid gloves."

Lars glared, but his gun went down from firing position.

Frank nodded. "Now, that's being reasonable. And I can be reasonable, too. I offer you a trade. My detonator for yours. Your boss's life for the briefcase bomb." He grinned without any humor in his eyes. "And I don't want to rush you, but I want it *now*. It shouldn't be so hard to make up your mind. I hear you guys make split-second decisions about human life all the time."

Lars glanced over at Habib, then at the Dutchman. Frank held his breath. This was the big gamble. He knew that the two hijackers were willing to die for the Dutchman. But would they sacrifice their own leader? Frank didn't think so—and he was risking his life on that hunch.

He knew that if the Dutchman could speak, he'd order his people to take out the whole plane. But the Dutchman had his mouth full right then.

Slowly, unwillingly, Lars's hand crept into his shirt pocket. He drew out a detonator that was almost a twin to the one Frank held.

"Good," said Frank. "Put it on the floor. And I'll put mine down."

They crouched to deposit the killer buttons, staring at each other, fingers on the triggers of their guns. This was the crucial part. If Lars got hold of both detonators, Frank and Joe would die. And Lars was convinced that the same would happen to him and Habib if Frank got both detonators.

"Okay." Frank's voice grew tighter as he gave the last instructions for the exchange. "Now we stand. Both of us step away from the detonators." They moved away. "Now, on the count of three, we pick up the one we want. One—two—three!"

Both of them pounced. Frank snatched up the

small electrical component, holding it tightly in his hand. He had done it! He had pulled the terrorists' fangs! This was their main threat to the airliner, and now it was neutralized. He almost went limp with relief, but still he kept a sharp eye on Lars.

"No!" Everyone's eyes shifted to Habib, who was backing up the aisle, his gun leveled at the group at the front of the plane—Frank, Joe, the Dutchman, and Lars. "We *need* the bomb," he said. "Our guns are not enough. Only the threat of the bomb will keep the policemen away."

He stared at Frank, sighting down his weapon. "You will put the detonator down," Habib said, almost parroting Frank's earlier instructions. "Then you will step away."

Frank opened his hand, studying the detonator for a long moment.

"Drop it, I say!" The ragged edge to Habib's voice was far more convincing than the volume he used.

Shrugging, Frank turned his hand, letting the detonator fall.

Passengers gasped or screamed as they saw the instrument of their destruction drop to the floor. Even Habib flinched, drawing back from the half-expected explosion.

When Habib jumped, his gun no longer covered the group. Frank used that second to complete phase two of his movement. He stomped on the detonator, crushing its radio microcircuits. Then he dove for the floor, praying that Joe would take his lead.

Habib shrieked in fury, triggering his Uzi. The hammering of rapid fire drowned him out as his bullets tore first into the ceiling, then sprayed randomly around the cabin. It also masked the cries of the passengers. They huddled on the floor as wild shots whizzed overhead.

Habib wasn't even aiming. He just swung his gun around in a wide arc, holding the trigger down. His fire was wild, the gun staying at shoulder height, sometimes rising above his head. Everyone on the plane had hit the floor, even the Dutchman. Somehow, Lars had pulled over the box that held the bound leader before the bullets started flying. Then he dove for cover.

Even though Habib's bullets had missed all human targets, they did do tremendous damage. The wild shots tore through the thin metal walls of the plane. They smashed lights, throwing sparks and fragments. And they shattered window after window.

Finally, Habib's forty-round clip ran out. He stood in the aisle, blinking in the sudden silence. The screaming had stopped. Only whimpers and a few terrified moans carried through the air.

Lying flat on the floor, Joe made some desperate calculations. Did he dare try a shot back at the terrorist? No, he didn't dare. Habib was standing right in the middle of the passengers.

Any off-target shot might hit an innocent by-stander. What if a stray bullet hit Callie?

If only he could run down there and take this guy on hand to hand. He'd beat him to a pulp!

But Habib was too far away. Before Joe could get halfway down the aisle, the terrorist would have the new clip in. Then it would be Joe who'd end up dead.

Joe sighed. He was still angry, but he wasn't stupid.

A new sound entered the airplane—the scream of sirens outside. Blinking red lights sparkled through the windows where Habib's bullets had torn through the shades and glass.

Habib ran down the aisle, hosing down the windows again with a new clip. "Stay away, police!" he screamed out the windows. By the time he was finished, the whole starboard side of the plane had lost all its windows. They seemed to explode as Habib's bullets hit them, flying outward in a hail of fragments.

Frank Hardy held his breath. What if the cops outside started firing back? They could leave the whole plane looking like Swiss cheese. He des-perately wished he had seen Callie before this all started happening. But before everything started, he hadn't had time to look. And now—well, if he stuck his head out, he'd probably get it blown off. Not that there'd be anything to see. All the passengers were hugging the floor. Even Habib's fellow hijacker was sprawled on the ground. Still, he'd like to see Callie, even if it was one last time—

The gunshots ended again—early, it seemed to Frank. He risked a quick peek, to find Habib muttering in his native tongue and smashing at the bolt on his Uzi. His gun had jammed!

Frank swung up, bringing his own gun to bear. Habib caught the motion and hurled his gun at Frank's head. While Frank ducked, Habib dug something out of the pocket of his pants.

He held it up before him in both hands. Frank froze. A grenade!

Habib's right thumb gripped the grenade, holding the handle in. His left thumb was hooked through the ring of the firing pin. One jerk, and the grenade would be armed. If he opened his right hand, the handle would fly off, the timer would begin, and ten seconds later the grenade would explode.

Frank shuddered to think of what the storm of shrapnel would do in an enclosed space.

Habib slowly walked forward, his eyes wide, madness behind them. "You destroyed our bomb. But I brought a bomb of my own, you see?" He actually had a smile on his face as he talked to Frank. "Now you, Mr. American Tough Guy, you get to die." Habib laughed wildly.

Right then, he passed Callie's seat. She wasn't in it, of course. Like everyone aboard the plane, she was crouched on the floor. And because she was a weak, nonthreatening woman, she was on the aisle.

From her vantage point, she couldn't see what Habib had in his hand. All she knew was that Habib had a weapon and that he was threatening Frank. So, as Habib came past, she did the only thing she could think of.

She tripped Habib.

His hands thrust out wildly as he lost his balance. The pin tore loose from the grenade and went flying. Habib managed to keep his grip on the grenade as he toppled forward, his eyes wide with terror.

Frank dashed forward as Habib hit the floor. The grenade was armed and trapped under the terrorist's body!

125

Chapter

16

HABIB LAY MOTIONLESS on the floor. He didn't even tremble. He was paralyzed with terror.

Frank Hardy was the only one who moved. He sprinted down the aisle of the airplane, dropping to his knees and skidding the last few feet. Before he had even stopped, he was flipping Habib over.

Frank took a long, deep breath of relief when he saw Habib's hand still tightly clenched around the grenade. "Okay," he said, reaching out his hand. "Just loosen up a bit. Give me that thing."

It was as though Habib hadn't even heard. He didn't move. He just lay where he was, glassy-eyed.

Frank took Habib's fist. The fingers wouldn't budge. He could break the grip if he broke the hand. But that wouldn't help much. If the handle

126

got loose, the bomb would be armed and ready to blast in seconds.

And even if he got the grenade with the handle still down, what would he do with it? Frank looked at the shape in Habib's hand. How weird to think that this small object, hardly larger than a baseball, could destroy the whole plane. Yet with the pin in, it was completely harmless.

That made up Frank's mind. The first thing to do was find the firing pin. With that back in, he could take the grenade from Habib.

Apparently, Habib realized what Frank was doing. That was when he came out of his funk. He gave Frank the grenade—right in the head, still clutched in his right fist.

It was a glancing blow, but hard enough to stun.

Frank reeled back, trying to blink away the jagged bolts of lightning that flashed before his eyes. Habib would be coming at him, trying to catch him while he was helpless.

The light show cleared enough to reveal a shadowy figure leaping at Frank, his arm raised for another blow. If he stayed where he was, Habib would probably nail him—permanently. In desperation, Frank threw himself forward at the figure.

They crashed into each other in the middle of the aisle, both on their knees now. Frank tried for a tackle to knock Habib down. He failed. Habib shoved him back, trying to butt Frank.

His forehead crashed into Frank's shoulder. They grappled together, Habib still flailing his right arm, trying to slug Frank with the grenade again.

Frank found himself fighting at a tremendous disadvantage. Habib had a wonderful weapon for trying to brain him. But even if Frank managed to disarm Habib, the live grenade would kill everyone on the plane.

They swayed back and forth in the aisle, lurching around as they tried to throw each other off balance. Then Habib sent them both crashing into one of the seats. Frank hit an armrest and lost his hold. Habib leaned back for a final blow, triumph on his face.

But that look soon turned to one of total shock and surprise. He made a horrible choking noise. Kneeling behind Habib, her face white and serious, was Callie. In her hands was the leather belt she had been wearing. But now Habib was wearing it—around his neck.

He tried hard to turn around, but Callie had a knee in his back. She tightened the belt, and instinctively both of Habib's hands went to his throat.

The grenade fell to the floor and bounced. The handle flew off. It was armed!

Frank darted forward, scooping up the bomb. It was no longer a question of putting the pin back in. There was just one crying need—to get the grenade off the plane. The seconds were ticking away. Frank rose to his feet, hurling the grenade out the nearest broken window. He didn't even have time to see what—or who—was out there.

"Watch out! Grenade!" he yelled, hoping the cops would be keeping pretty far away. They must have been pretty confused by then about what was happening on board the jetliner.

The blast from outside was far away, but it still shook the plane. Frank paid no attention. He still had a job to take care of. Pivoting around, he threw a karate blow at Habib. He was just in time. The hijacker had managed to squirm around to grab at Callie. The blow landed with devastating force. Frank was through playing around with this guy, especially since his metallic hot potato was gone.

The blow tore Habib away from Callie. The terrorist caromed into one of the seats, then bounced off to hit the floor.

Frank dropped to his knees to pick Habib up. As he fell, a new volley of bullets flew over his head. Frank turned to see Lars whipping his Uzi around one-handed as Joe dropped to the floor for cover. With his free hand, the terrorist dragged the bound figure of the Dutchman, and they retreated into the first-class cabin.

Once again, everyone hugged the floor until the two terrorists were out of sight. But Frank was busy even as the bullets flew. He threw a choke hold on Habib—this one wasn't getting away. The hijacker thrashed for a few seconds. But as the shooting stopped, his body dropped like a deflated balloon. The Hardys may have lost two of the bad guys, but the third was definitely out of the game.

Joe stood up, his face twisted in a scowl. "Real cute. He fired low enough to keep me from interfering with him and just high enough to reward me for being a good boy."

Frank nodded. He knew that if Joe had tried to stop Lars, the terrorist would have aimed low, killing Joe and probably maiming dozens of innocent passengers.

"At least we've got them now," Joe said. "They're trapped in the nose of the plane. They know that if they try coming back here again, they'll be walking into our guns. If they try to get off the plane—well, that's what all those cops outside are waiting for."

Frank nodded. "They've got big problems. This plane is going nowhere, and they're about to lose their hostages."

A babble of noise erupted from the crowd of passengers.

"What do you mean?" A woman's voice cut across the noise.

Frank turned to her, staring for a second. Then he realized why she looked familiar. Despite the stringy hair and the bags under her eyes, this was Pauline Fox.

"The hijackers control the front hatch of the plane," he explained. "That's where passengers usually get on or off. But there are escape hatches in the tail."

"They could shoot us as we get off!" the newswoman said.

"We'll call to the cops first," said Frank. "Tell them what's going on in here. Then they can lay cover fire on the nose of the plane—keep the terrorists' heads down until everyone is off and safe. But first things first."

Frank looked down at Habib, lying at his feet. "We need something to tie this guy up with." He turned to his brother. "And we need somebody to cover that front doorway. Joe, that's a job for you and your gun. See if you can find stuff to make a barricade. Everyone else, go back to your seats. Don't sit down. Stay on the floor. We'll need somebody from the plane crew to open those hatches."

He grinned at Callie. "And I'd like you to come with me. We'll give the cops the good news, together."

The passengers listened to these plans in a happy daze. They had spent so much time in mortal danger, they could hardly believe that they were safe now.

They weren't.

As two flight attendants opened the rear

hatches, the whole plane began to tremble. A high-pitched whine filled the cabin—a whine that anyone who had ever flown was sure to recognize. It was just louder because so many of the windows were gone.

It was the sound of jet engines starting up.

The airliner jolted as it started moving forward, nearly throwing Frank and Callie out the emergency hatch.

"Lars—the tall blond—said he was good at mechanical stuff," Callie said. "He just never mentioned that he knew how to fly one of these."

Joe threw himself through the door into first-class and was met by a quick burst of fire. He jumped back to friendly territory. "The Dutchman's standing guard with the Uzi," he reported. "Looks like they piled up all the carry-on luggage in first-class to barricade the door to the cockpit."

Frank looked out one of the shattered windows. "We're moving too fast to let people jump off," he said.

"What I don't get is why they're doing this," Joe complained. "I mean, they can keep us aboard until they run out of fuel—" He jerked as the plane lurched through another turn. "You know, this Lars guy doesn't strike me as a very good pilot."

"Good enough," one of the flight attendants said in a tight voice. "He's taxiing out to one of the runways. If he's good enough to do that, he's good enough to get us into the air."

She stared at the broken windows. "And the cockpit has its own air system."

Everyone's eyes went to the windows in slow horror.

"Those guys will have a chance to escape and air to breathe," Callie said quietly. "But when the plane rises high enough, those broken windows will let all the air out of here. All of us will suffocate!"

Chapter

17

THE PASSENGERS BEGAN to crowd into the aisle, completely giving way to panic. Cries and screams filled the air, fighting with the whine of the jet engines. But the engine noise still dominated, growing louder as the plane picked up speed.

Even though there was nowhere to go, people began pushing at one another. Then they began shoving and clawing. Some of the more desperate people began heading for the rear escape hatches. Better to jump to a possible death than stay aboard for a sure one.

Callie looked nervously at Frank as the crowd headed their way. They were standing right in front of the hatches, directly in the path of what was rapidly becoming a mob.

Frank's face was cold and remote. Callie knew

that look. Frank was running over about a dozen possible plans to get them out of this. And from the frown on his face, she could tell none of them would work.

Before the crowd got to within pushing distance, however, Frank snapped back to the real world. He turned his frown on the mob.

"Out of our way!" screamed a heavyset woman. Her hair looked like a wad of collapsed cotton candy. Only its orange color helped Frank and Callie recognize Mrs. Thayer, the senator's wife. "You can't keep us here! We aren't going to stay and die like rats in a trap!"

"You can't jump from a moving plane," Frank told her. "It's like leaping from a second-story window."

But those people weren't ready to discuss anything rationally. More and more passengers pushed against those in the front ranks. They began advancing on Frank and Callie. "Let us off! Let us off!"

Frank shook his head in disbelief. But as hands grabbed for him, he shoved Callie behind him. "Don't be stupid!" he shouted.

Then a new chant rose from the back of the group. "Throw them off! Throw them out!"

For a second, Frank stared. He shouted to the people, but they were making too much noise for him to be heard. He glanced at the weapon in his hand, and then he used it. A quick burst into the ceiling shocked the crowd into silence.

"Look, all of you. This plane has two engines—both of them in the tail and both of them over these hatches."

"So what?" somebody called.

"Remember how a jet crashed some years ago because a flock of starlings got sucked into the air intakes for the engines?" Frank asked. "Those intakes are right up there." He pointed over his head.

"We don't have many starlings handy," a voice said.

"No, but we've got blankets, paper, pillows, and magazines." Frank stared into the faces of the crowd. "If we can starve those jets of air, we won't take off. It's a better gamble than jumping thirty feet onto the runway."

"He's right," another voice cried out.

"Yeah. Let's get that junk up here!"

"Come on!"

"Form a line," Frank called. "Pass the stuff along. And cut up the big stuff, like the blankets. We want it small enough to get sucked in but big enough to stick."

He shouted up to the front of the cabin. "Joe, you stay on guard duty."

"Just what I've *been* doing," Joe called back. "While you were busy discussing policy with that lynch mob."

With a chance to do something to save themselves, the passengers went to work feverishly.

Mrs. Thayer led the group in charge of tearing

up the blankets. Her hairdo wobbled ridiculously as she reduced the blankets to long strips. "Ow!" she cried. "Third nail I've broken so far!" But she kept on tearing.

Pauline Fox was searching through the seats, trying to find more things to throw into the engines. "Not my bag!" a woman cried as she picked up a canvas tote.

"Honey, it's not going to be much use to you if we go up there." She dumped the bag onto a seat and passed it up the line, shaking her head. "The best story of my life, and I don't have a camera handy."

"If you did, we'd be passing that up, too!" somebody called.

Callie and Frank grinned at each other as they stood at the end of one line, tossing stuff as high as they could, past the jet intakes. "Look at all this—stuff," Frank grunted as he hurled torn blankets up.

"I like this," Callie replied, tossing a set of plastic cards Frisbee-style into the engine. "They're the instructions on what to do in case of an emergency."

Frank grinned at her. "Well, this is an emergency, isn't it?"

The flood of items began to decrease as the searchers reached the seats at the back. Then it swelled as they started going over the cabin again, scavenging in new and more creative ways. Pauline Fox ripped the headrest covers off the seats. Mrs. Thayer and her crew started tearing the elastic magazine holders from the seats.

"Hey, look what I found!" Professor Beemis called out. "The bag that terrorist was using to make his collection."

"My money!" somebody else cried.

"My pearls!" shouted a woman.

"Pass it up," said Frank.

"*What?*" a roar of furious voices demanded.

"The money is paper, just like the magazine pages," Frank said. "And the metal in the jewelry will do a real job on the vanes in the engine."

"Expensive paper," one of the passengers muttered.

"It'll all be worthless if we don't live to spend it," said Frank. He opened his own wallet, took out the bills, and tossed them into the intake. "Anybody else?"

Everyone feverishly searched pockets and purses. Money, handkerchiefs, even used tissues appeared on the line.

Habib's bag of loot came up to Frank and Callie. They tossed handfuls of bills up at the jet intake.

"If these things go through, they'll make the airport people very happy," Callie said.

"Probably look more like confetti than money," Frank said.

"This had better start working soon," Professor Beemis called out. "We've reached the runway now."

Stuff began appearing at a fever pitch as the plane prepared for its leap into the air. Callie and Frank found themselves throwing trays snapped from the chairs, seat belts, even people's shirts torn off and handed up the line.

The jet engines revved faster. "Lars is preparing for his takeoff." Callie gritted her teeth.

A low groan went through the group of passengers.

"Wait a second! What's that noise?" asked Mrs. Thayer, shushing everyone.

They all listened intently. There it came again—a clunk, a rasping sound that grew into a loud grinding noise. The whole plane began to shake wildly. Then the whine of the jets died away. The airliner coasted along until it came to a stop, about two-thirds of the way down the runway.

"There's smoke coming from one of the engines," Professor Beemis reported, craning his neck out the window. "And the most unbelievable trail of garbage you ever saw, stretched out behind us."

The passengers whistled and cheered. From the distance came the sound of sirens as police cars raced to barricade the runway. The airport's fire engines and crash trucks came roaring up, too.

"They gave it their best shot, but we beat them," Callie said. "We've won!"

"Not so fast!" a voice called from the first-

139

class area. It was the Dutchman. "I have something you should see. Will you allow me into your cabin?"

"What's up, pal?" called Joe. "You want to surrender?"

"Let us just say I want to end this," the Dutchman shouted back. "I promise, no gun play. Here." A harsh black shape came flying through the doorway, clattering to the floor. Lars's Uzi.

"We've got Habib's gun, and the Dutchman is clean," Joe said. "Unless Lars is toting a pistol in his back pocket."

He shrugged. "We'll be ready for him." Stepping back and well to the side, Joe aimed his machine gun to cover the door.

"Okay, Dutchman," Frank yelled. "Come on in."

The pudgy figure of the head terrorist appeared in the doorway. "Wrecking the engines to ruin our escape." He shook his head. "I would never have thought of that. I'm afraid you've destroyed an International Airways plane, however." The Dutchman shrugged his shoulders, lifting up the briefcase he held in his right hand.

"Why don't you put that case down?" Frank said. "I want to see what you've got hidden in your other hand."

"Oh, gladly," said the Dutchman. He put the case down at his feet. In his left hand he held—Frank's detonator.

"This is the bomb we brought aboard. And I

think you know what I have in my hand." The terrorist's voice was almost gentle, as if he were lecturing on a minor subject.

"You thought you were so smart, trading your detonator for ours." Now the Dutchman's voice hardened. "Using a different frequency to set your bomb off. You were *too* smart. Lars and I built a new detonating charge, using the plastique you crammed into my mouth. I won't be captured and made a fool of."

He raised his hand, his thumb poised over the blasting button. "You see, it doesn't matter that you destroyed this plane. Because I will finish the job."

Chapter

18

CALLIE THREW HER arms around Frank, holding him close. They were just too far away to do anything.

Joe Hardy threw away his gun and hurtled himself at the Dutchman.

"Fool!" sneered the terrorist. He pressed the button on his detonator.

Nothing happened.

The Dutchman gawked at his hand. He pressed the button twice more—three times. Then he went for the briefcase bomb.

But Joe was standing in front of him. "You were pretty brave with that bomb at your feet. Ready to blow us all to kingdom come. Let's see how well you do with *these* bombs." He raised his fists.

"Now this one I call the Big Bang—" He

rammed his left fist into the Dutchman's paunch. The terrorist gasped and folded in half, still clicking away with the detonator.

"And this one I call the Big Boom. Now I'm going to lower it on you." Joe brought his right fist down on top of the Dutchman's head. The terrorist crashed to the floor.

"All right, Joe, that's enough. He's lost it all, and he knows it. Let it go at that." Frank came down the aisle to join his younger brother.

"Uh-uh," said Joe. He reached for the briefcase. "I'm going to open this and feed him every flavor of plastique that's in there. And I'll make sure he swallows it all."

"No way." Frank put his foot on top of the case. "For all we know, they may have a booby-trap set in this so it explodes if it's opened. Leave him for the cops."

Callie stood beside Frank. "That was really something," she said to Joe. "Jumping him like that. It's almost as if you knew the bomb wouldn't go off."

"Well," said Joe, trying to look modest and heroic.

Frank laughed. "He *did* know the bomb wouldn't go off. So did I. Right after the Dutchman said he had used the plastique we'd stuck in his mouth to make the detonating charge."

"What?" Callie whirled around.

"Come on, Callie." Frank grinned. "Where were we going to find any plastic explosive?

143

Frank did have a little CN stuck to his hand after our fight with Lonnie, this crew's bomb maker. But not enough to do anything useful.''

"Sure, it was useful," Joe cut in. "I was able to match the exact same color and texture with the modeling clay I bought when you sent me out.''

"M-m-modeling clay?" Callie sputtered.

"Yeah. Looked like CN, felt like CN— 'Course, it didn't *taste* like CN. But then, I guess our friend here never tried nibbling on any of his bombs.''

Callie was still in shock. "You mean, you had him thinking it was a bomb, and all along it was modeling clay in his mouth?''

"You got it." Frank's eyes twinkled as he grinned.

The Dutchman made a strangling sound down on the floor.

"Sounds like he's still got it," said Joe. "Maybe he's got some caught on his tonsils." He went over and picked up his gun. "And now, if you'll excuse me, I have to go to visit our friend Lars.''

Apparently, Lars had lost all his fight when the big explosion failed to come. Moments later, they could hear Joe's voice over the last remaining loudspeakers. "This is your honorary captain speaking. The last terrorist has surrendered, and I've just spoken with the police. They're moving a set of passenger stairs up to the front hatch.

Why don't you start lining up to get off this crate?'' He laughed. ''At least there won't be much in the way of luggage!''

The passengers burst into excited chatter at the thought of finally escaping from the plane. Mrs. Thayer started trying to pat her hair into order.

Pauline Fox stopped beside Callie and Frank. ''I want to thank you, kids. First for saving my life. And second for giving me the story of my career! Wait till I catch up with my camera crew. If this doesn't win me an award—'' She shook their hands and joined the line.

As the passengers started filing forward, several stopped to thank the kids. ''I don't even know your names, and you saved us all,'' one woman said.

''We *all* worked together to save ourselves. If you hadn't helped stop those engines . . .'' Frank smiled and shook his head.

''Well, won't you at least go out ahead of us?'' another passenger asked.

Again, Frank shook his head. ''I think the cops might get nervous if they saw anybody coming out of the plane with a machine gun. Besides, we still have these goons to guard.''

''We'll take care of them,'' a voice from behind him said.

Frank turned around to find Roger O'Neill clambering through the escape hatch. ''We set up a ladder back here,'' the government man explained. He moved a little stiffly, as if he had a bad set of bruises.

A crew of policemen followed O'Neill. And after them came Fenton Hardy, with a look of fury on his face.

"Uh-oh," Frank heard Joe whisper as he came to turn Lars over to the cops. "We're in trouble now."

Fenton Hardy crossed his arms across his chest, glaring at his sons. "It's not enough that you run off like a pair of vigilantes when my back is turned. But then, after I specifically ordered you—"

"They did save us, Mr. Hardy," Callie said, cutting in desperately. "They saved everybody on the plane."

"I can understand your gratitude to these two," Fenton Hardy said to her. "What I can't understand is how they expected—"

"Actually, Fenton, if you're going to blame anyone, it should be me." Agent O'Neill looked as if saying those words hurt him even more than his bruises. "I recruited them after we left the Hole-in-the-Wall. Because so many of the ANWO terrorists were young people, I thought they might be able to infiltrate the group. Everything they did—*everything*—was under my orders."

Frank and Joe stared at the Espionage Resources agent. Why was he lying to get them off the hook? Frank had been expecting O'Neill to have them thrown in jail.

Then the answer appeared from the crowd of cops behind O'Neill. A man in an airport security guard's uniform turned around. He was an ordinary sort, the kind of guy who disappears in a crowd. But this guy winked at the Hardys.

It was the Gray Man.

Frank and Joe immediately got the message. A little more interagency politics, a deal cut between Espionage Resources and the Network. And, although Espionage Resources might get the credit on TV, the Hardys suspected that the people who counted would know that Network agents had really gotten the job done.

"Actually," Frank said to O'Neill, "I hope you can keep our names out of this. We worked under your orders, so you should really be the hero."

"Oh," said O'Neill. "Um. Well, I suppose we can arrange something like that." He began to smile. "I will need a final report, though, before we go public with the story of the rescue."

"Sure," said Frank. "And there's one other person to be picked up." He gave the address of the house near Sheridan Circle. "There's a girl tied up in the living room—Olympia Morrison. She was our contact to the Dutchman."

"Good, good. Fine. Where is our press officer?" O'Neill asked.

"I guess I owe you boys an apology," Fenton Hardy said. "Your actions are much more understandable now that I know you were working with

147

Agent O'Neill.'' He glared at the government man. "You might have told me.''

"Sorry, Fenton,'' said O'Neill, lying desperately. "It was on a need-to-know basis only. You might have tried to get involved. We couldn't risk it.''

"Well,'' said Fenton Hardy. "I want you boys to promise me one thing. You won't do any more work for these people. Okay?''

"Okay, Dad,'' the Hardys promised. "We won't do any work for Espionage Resources.''

The Gray Man smiled and disappeared into the crowd.

"Now, what's all this about a girl?'' Callie wanted to know.

"Oh, it was terrible, Callie,'' Joe said. "We both tried to romance this girl to find out where the secret headquarters was. And I—'' He hung his head. "I struck out. She wanted nothing to do with me. She wanted a dashing man of action— like Frank here.''

"Oh yeah?'' Callie's hands were on her hips.

"It's not the way it sounds,'' Frank said, beginning to explain.

"Really?'' said Callie.

"I told you,'' Joe said with a grin. "You should have stuck with Pia and quit while you were ahead.''

He quickly retreated as Callie glared at him.

Frank and Callie stood staring at each other in the now-empty plane.

"You know," Callie finally said, "sometimes you can be a real jerk."

"There was nothing going on with Pia," Frank said. "She wound up trying to shoot me—twice."

"I know that," Callie said. "I was wondering how long you were going to wait before you kissed me."

Frank didn't need a second invitation.

Moments later, they headed out of the plane together, laughing.

"Remind me to rescue you more often," Frank said.

"Don't hold your breath," Callie retorted. "After this adventure, I just want a good long rest."

"The seminar will be over soon," Frank said. "Then we'll hop a plane home—"

"No way!" Callie cut him off. "You can come along with me if you want, but I'm telling you right now, I'm going home *by bus*."

Frank shrugged. "Okay, Greyhound, here we come. But if somebody wants to take the bus to Havana—"

Be sure to read
all the books in the
Hardy Boys Casefiles Series: